CW01650099

Cold Storage

Cover art copyright © 2000, 2001 by Mike Bohatch - Mike@eyesofchaos.com
Introduction copyright © 2000 by Graham Masterton
"Scoring" copyright © 2000 by Carl Hose
"Parts" copyright © 2000 by Walt Hicks
"The Calling" copyright © 2000 by Paul Melniczek
"Angel killer" copyright © 2000 by Horns
"Dining at Sea" copyright © 2000 by Steven E. Wedel
"Rampart" copyright © 2000 by Amy Grech
"The Hotel of the Dead" copyright © 2000 by Kevin James Miller
"Expiation" copyright © 2000 by L.J. Blount
"After the Fall" copyright © 2000 by Paul Fry

Edited by Paul Fry

Additional editing by Carl Hose.
Introduction by Graham Masterton

ISBN 1-929072-67-8

Published 2001

Published by Short, Scary Tales Publications, 15 North Roundhay, Stechford, Birmingham, B33 9PE, England. ©2000, 2001 Paul Fry. All rights reserved. No part of this publication may be reproduced, stored in a retrieval system, or transmitted in any form or by any means, electronic, mechanical, recording or otherwise, without the prior written permission of the publisher.

Manufactured in England.

The characters and events in this book are fictitious. Any similarity to real persons, living or dead, is coincidental and not intended by the author.

Booklocker.com, Inc.
2001

Cold Storage

Edited by Paul Fry

Cold Storage

They drifted quietly for a while. Raymond kept looking at the box, trying to figure out what was wrong with it. Finally he realized what he'd been looking for.

"There's no nails or screws in the top of this box," he said. He reached out and pushed at the top panel, but it didn't move. "How do you think it's fastened?"

"I don't care," Manuel said. "I am getting hungry. Maybe I will cut a piece at a time to keep you alive until I have to kill you. I like my meat to be fresh. I could cut off a leg below the knee tonight, the other tomorrow, then the arms—"

—From "Dining at Sea" by Steven E. Wedel

Dedication

For

Carol Fry.

Thank you for being the best mother anyone could wish for.

Love you always,

Paul.

x

Acknowledgements

When the idea for this anthology first came to me one dark and rainy night in England last May (actually, it was light and sunny, but that doesn't have the same effect, does it?), I didn't think that anything would come of it. But after I started to approach the authors with the idea, I realized that it just might work.

I started receiving the first stories about 3-4 weeks later and I knew that this would be a great book.

The next step was to get the cover art designed. My first choice was for a great artist that I had dealt with before. I contacted him and asked him if he would be interested in doing the cover art for this anthology. He said that he would, and then set about designing the artwork.

I'd like to send a big, big thank you to Mike Bohatch for all of his time and hard work. The cover is amazing, Mike.

Most importantly, I would like to thank the authors that contributed a tale to this book. Your creative and disturbed minds (only kidding guys!) have been working overtime, trying to conjure-up the most original and scary tales.

You have definitely succeeded. The stories are great. Without you, this book would not exist. Thank you.

Thanks also to Walt Hicks and Carl Hose for all of your help with this book. I know I must have drove you crazy with my constant emails asking for help.

I'd also like to say a very special thank you to my friend Carl Hose for editing my story and for showing me how proper grammar is supposed to be. Thank you Carl, it's much appreciated.

And a very special thank you to Graham Masterton for writing the introduction to this book. It means a great deal to us all.

And lastly, thank *you* very much for buying this book. I hope you have lots of fun reading it.

Sit back . . . clear your mind . . . and let the nightmare begin....

Paul Fry,
Editor.

1st of August 2000.

CONTENTS

Introduction

When I first became old enough to read horror stories, there were hardly any horror stories to read. There was Frankenstein, of course, and Dracula, and the various Satanic works of Dennis Wheatley, as well as the Pan Book of Horror Stories, edited by the late Herbert van Thal. But for an avid young reader with a lurid imagination, the selection was very limited and I quickly found that I had devoured almost every blood-curdling story that was available in print.

I managed to find a backstreet newsagent which sold American horror comics, which in those days were brought over to Britain as ballast in merchant-ships, and it was through these that I first discovered some of the more horrifying urban legends, such as The Heap...a pile of rags and rubbish which took on human life and dismembered its careless creator. In fact I liked The Heap so much that I have made a passing reference to it in one of my newer novels, Swimmer.

When the horror comics dried up, there was nothing for it but to write my own horror stories. I wrote a new one every day, after my homework, and read them the following morning to my friends at school. I met one of those friends only a year ago—these days he's a merchant banker—and he admitted that he had nightmares for years about an opera singer who had been decapitated in a car accident and whose headless body wandered the opera house every night, bubbling out Nessun Dorma.

My most important discovery was that horror stories didn't have to be set in Transylvania, in bat-infested castles; or even in that distorted world that travelers enter when they take the wrong fork in the woods in Lovecraft-land. The protagonists didn't have to be noblemen like the Duke De Richelieu or experts in vampirism like Dr Van Helsing. They could be ordinary people leading mundane lives who suddenly find themselves confronted by something deeply disturbing and strange beyond all imagination.

Like Harry Erskine, in The Manitou, who finds a Native American medicine-man being reborn on the back of a woman's neck. He's nothing but a chancer, neither rich nor famous, but making a living by telling fortunes to gullible old ladies. Other characters have included plumbers, restaurateurs, librarians, shopkeepers, local newspaper reporters...all of them unprepared for the terror that is about to be unleashed on them.

By visiting horror on everyday people, I found that it could be far richer, far more diverse, and far more plausible...even if I was asking the reader to suspend his or her disbelief to breaking point.

In this anthology, Cold Storage, we can find writers searching for that same plausibility, and introducing horror mostly through characters with whom we can identify...even when we can't completely sympathize with them. It shows that new writers are working hard to keep the genre alive, and to push forward the envelope of fear.

I wish them all the very best, and look forward to seeing each of them develop and flourish in the future.

Graham Masterton

Cork, Ireland

Scoring by Carl Hose

A girl ambles toward me. She must have been beautiful once . . . before she became one of them. Now her blonde hair is filthy with grave dirt and her complexion is like clay. She died young, I can see that much. Late teens, maybe early twenties. Judging by the ragged line I see around her neck, I imagine she met the wrong end of a knife. Maybe a jealous boyfriend went nuts and cut her throat for cheating on him. Maybe just some weird psycho in a dark alley. Those were the days, though, when all we had to worry about was your standard everyday psycho. Shit ain't that easy anymore.

Not since the goddamn death plague.

I watch the chick make her way toward my cabin, stopping when she reaches the fresh dead body between us. You have to use some sort of distraction to play the game. Scoring is dangerous without something to occupy the dead bitches. I know people who try to score without using a distraction, but it just ain't a healthy situation, if you know what I mean.

The dead girl takes the bait. She'll be easy, I can see that already. She kneels over the corpse and bends down to eat from the open wound in its stomach, pausing now and again to lick the blood from her thin, crusted lips. Her attention is completely focused. She won't even know I'm there. I can score and be gone before she even finishes her meal.

I'm careful as I walk toward her. The damn things can be a little testy sometimes. I pause every so often, making sure she keeps on eating. I walk right up to her. She watches me as I get a little closer, but she keeps right on digging through the bloody contents of the dead body's stomach, stuffing intestines into her mouth like fresh sausage.

She's wearing a dress. That makes it easier. Trying to get pants off the walking dead is hard work. Takes up a lot of your time, which don't leave much left over for the actual score.

I'm the scoring champ in my area, I ever tell you that? Well . . . it's true enough. There's a couple of guys I know ain't too bad, but none of them ever came close to topping my record. I once scored twelve times in one day.

Anyway, so I'm going up to this dead bitch now. She's occupied. I lift her dress and take down her dirty panties. She glances back at me real quick, like I'm just a minor irritation or something. Mainly she just cares about the food in front of her—all that stringy, bloody meat dangling from her lips like spaghetti.

I never kiss these things. You don't know where they've put their mouth. Kissing is one thing a fella learns to live without nowadays.

The zombie bitch has a surprisingly tight little pussy on her. Cold but tight. I stick my dick in and start to fuck her. Maybe it's just wishful thinking on my part, but I swear she wiggled her clay-gray ass back against me a time or two. Like she was enjoying it, I mean.

I finish with my dead little slut just as the corpse she's feeding on opens its eyes. That's what you got to watch out for with a fresh corpse. They're dead one minute, next thing you know, you got the son of a bitch coming after you.

I hurry back to my cabin and grab my shotgun. I shoot my little fuck friend first, then I blast the other one. Get them in the head and you can be sure they stay dead. Once you do that, you want to burn the bodies for that extra bit of assurance.

So I fetch a can of gasoline from the shed, douse both corpses, then toss a match on the things and watch them turn to ash.

That's all she wrote.

I go back into the cabin, shut the door, and throw the bolt. I'm safe here. The windows are covered with thick pieces of wood and layered with scrap metal. Those things aren't very strong. Sometimes at night, they scratch and push at the door, but they ain't got the strength to get through my barricade. It's annoying. I've learned to live with it. Used to scare hell out of me at first, but I take it in stride now. I know they eventually give up and wander about their business.

I stoke the fireplace and pour myself a shot of whiskey. I still got a lot of good whiskey left, thank god.

I feel good. I always feel good after I score.

I didn't use to do it, you know. Thought it was a disgusting sport first time I heard of it. Screwing dead things just didn't seem proper, even if they was moving around.

Times change, though, and a man has to make some serious choices. Things are just too crazy now, what with zombies being the dominant nationality and all. It's hard to find a live person to fuck, and to be honest, not really worth the effort. I'd just as soon stick my dick in some walking corpse and be done with it. Once I came to realize that the way it is now is the way it's always going to be, I decided to give scoring a try, and hell, I been hooked ever since. Like I said, I'm the best there is in this neck of the woods.

Scoring truly does relieve stress. Everybody seems to be doing it these days. It's sort of a national pastime. Maybe even worldwide, I don't know. I ain't a traveler. The only time I go out is to score. Other than that, I'd just as soon stay in my cabin and drink my whiskey. It's just too goddamn insane out there for me, if you know what I mean.

I used to jerk off a lot, back before I got into scoring. Still got a couple magazines left over from when life was normal.

That first time I scored—ahhh, the memories. They say you never forget your first. Mine was a cheerleader. Found her wandering the streets in town. She still looked pretty damn fresh. Couldn't have been dead more than a few hours. I watched her amble on over to a dead dog and start feeding on it, chomping on the guts, down on her hands and knees, her pretty little face buried in its stomach. Seeing that ass all raised up like it was, I couldn't resist. I was scared as hell, but I went for it. I snuck up there and yanked her little white panties down and started doing her. Just like that, I got me a piece of that chick, and believe me, it felt good.

Submissive babes.

The walking dead give that concept a whole new meaning. They don't complain. You can fuck them all night if you want, long as you keep a lot of distractions on hand.

I do miss blow jobs, though. That's one thing you don't get these days. Not from a score, anyways. Sticking your dick in a zombie's mouth is like spoon feeding it. Try it if you want, but I ain't responsible for the outcome.

I hear something outside. I think it's one of them—wait a minute, I hear a voice. It's a female voice. She's calling for help.

I move quickly to the door, slide open the peephole, and take a look outside. Sure enough, there's a woman out there, standing right on my porch, banging away at the door.

A *live* woman.

She keeps glancing over her shoulder, frantic as a couple of rotten corpses lurch toward her. I throw the bolt, open the door, and drag the girl inside.

She thanks me as she throws her arms around my neck and starts sobbing on my shoulder.

My cabin is in the mountains, away from town. It's away from just about everything. I briefly wonder what brought the woman to my door, but I decide not to ask. Think I'll just consider it a gift of the Gods.

I offer her whiskey. It's all I have. She's grateful for it. She's a bit calmer after she drinks a shot of it.

One of the dead things begins to scratch at my door. The woman panics again.

I tell her they can't get in. She seems pleased by the news. She relaxes again, thanking me profusely for saving her ass. She wonders what she can ever do to repay me.

I ask her how she feels about giving blow jobs. . . .

Weeks have gone by. The dead don't make it up here as often as they used to. There are times when days pass without one of them stumbling by.

The girl—Sally—has begun to get on my nerves. She gives good blow jobs, but they ain't worth the hassle of living with her. Thought I'd like it, having a live girl around and all. I figured it would be nice to fuck something that fucked back. I especially looked forward to feeling a soft, wet mouth on my dick again.

It was at first, but the honeymoon is over. The girl talks too much. Mostly bitching. I can't stand it, I tell you. I mean, the dead ones never talked back. That was part of the pleasure.

I miss scoring. What I wouldn't give to get back to the challenge of the sport.

Sally's going at it again, yapping about this, yapping about that. I watch her sweet little mouth as she complains about the state of things. She sounds like a fucking poodle.

I'll miss her blow jobs, but like I said, they ain't worth the hassle.

I offer her a shot of whiskey. That's another thing I hate. The bitch is drinking up my whiskey. This one is different, though. I put in a bit of poison—a little something left over from the days when I had a rat problem. The rats are gone now. The zombies like to snack in between meals. There's only one use for the poison now; she's sitting in my cabin.

Rat poison is a good way to do it. Much better than hacking her head off or blowing her heart out with my shotgun. This way, you see, she looks presentable when she comes back.

I'll build a special little room to keep her in. No more blow jobs, but, hell, at least I'll be able to score anytime I get the urge. . . .

Parts by Walt Hicks

Andrew "Parts" Parkins sat patiently in the sleek black BMW 740iL sedan drumming his fingers on the leather-wrapped steering wheel. It was almost one a.m. and most of the city was asleep, except for the night crawlers. He was roughly juxtaposed between the city's two major hospitals—Mercy General and Good Hope. That's what he liked most about his job, you never knew where you might be headed.

The cool, ghastly-silent air conditioning embraced him; he swigged from an Evian bottle. He mentally calmed his blood pressure, respiration, and metabolism to near nil, conserving his energies in anticipation of the call he was sure would come tonight. Parkins was dressed in an inexpensive, though tasteful black suit, plain silk tie knotted immaculately at his throat. He was a near-perfect physical specimen; daily workouts, the proper diet, no smoke, drink or drug entered the temple of his body. In his business, he had seen all too often the horrific bodily damage, both internal and external, caused by man's own stupidity and carelessness. Parkins wanted to live a long, long time, but in good health, not a disease-ridden, emaciated husk of his younger self.

The Motorola cell phone chirped quietly in the chill silence. Parkins pressed a button on the unit attached to his belt, activating the headset he wore.

"Go," he said.

"Andrew?" his wife Angela's thin, wan voice unexpectedly queried.

"You stupid bitch," Parkins growled, disappointment shattering his self-imposed calm. "I've told you a thousand fucking times not to call me when I'm working."

"It's Travis, Andrew." Her tired, quiet voice was on the edge of panic. Travis was their seven-month-old son, practically the only thing in Parkins' life he even remotely cared about, other than making money.

"What?" Parkins was exasperated.

"He hasn't stopped crying tonight. He has a one hundred-degree temperature." Angela's voice broke ever so slightly.

"What the fuck do you want me to do? Call the goddamn doctor. Or better yet, take him to the emergency room. I am ***working***, Angela. For Christ's Sake, do I have to make every fucking move for you?"

Parkins swatted the disconnect button, cutting off the annoying sound of Angela softly weeping. He took a deep, cleansing breath, attempting to regain his lost calm. The cell chirped once again.

"Speak," he barked, thinking it was Angela again.

"Good evening to you, too, Parts." It was his boss, Mr. William Calisto.

The smile in Calisto's voice told Parkins something good was working tonight. "Whasssuuuup, Boss?"

Calisto chuckled. "Ready to do the deed, my man?"

"Now, when has the kid ever let you down, Slick?" Parkins called his boss 'Slick' because Calisto was originally from Arkansas and could do a frighteningly plausible President Clinton impersonation.

"Damn near never, Parts." There was genuine admiration in Calisto's voice. And something akin to awe.

"Whatcha got, Slick?" Parkins asked around a smile. He switched on the headlights and slipped the BMW into gear.

"En route to Good Hope, 21-year-old male, motorcycle accident. Sounds like a terminal head injury. Parents are on their way. We could score huge on this one, Parts."

Parkins was already wheeling the BMW along the familiar route to Good Hope Hospital. He would get there before the ambulance. The adrenaline was pumping. "Yeah, big time. Any history on the road kill?"

"No, need you to get that info and get back to me. With the backlogs we have, should be no problem for a positive harvest."

An emaciated stray dog stumbled out onto the street in front of the speeding BMW. Parkins swerved a bit, catching the dog beneath the right front tire. He heard a single, painful yelp, then the satisfying thumpa-thumpa as the dog perished beneath the BMW. Perfect. No dents, no scratches, probably not even blood spray on the body of the car. It was going to be a good night.

"Sounds good, Slick. I'll intercept the parents while the docs are doing their thing. Any familial background?"

"Nothing. But that wouldn't be any fun for you, anyway, would it?" Parkins could 'hear' Calisto grinning.

"Not a problem. Well, I'm off to nail down my kid's college education."

"You da man, Parts. You ***da man!***"

Parkins wheeled into a parking space near the emergency room entrance of Good Hope Hospital. It was marked 'Clergy Only' so Parkins dangled a cleric's parking pass from his rear view mirror. He checked his look in the rear-view, straightened his silk tie and smiled at himself. His countenance melded into a look of genuine concern, his brow furrowing compassionately. "Mr. and Mrs. 'Fill in the blank', I am so sorry for your loss. My name is Andrew Parkins with Life Longevity . . ." His face was abruptly painted a wild, hellish red. The ambulance had arrived. He pointed his index finger at his reflection in the mirror. "Show time!"

Andrew Parkins was well-known by the emergency room staff at both Good Hope and Mercy General Hospitals. Life Longevity, Inc. was an officially government-registered OPO—Organ Procurement Organization. The presumably non-for-profit organization was one of the most efficiently run, administratively conscientious of the lot and it seemed that Andrew Parkins was consistently on-scene whenever availability for possible organ donation presented itself. But Parkins had the reputation as one of the most compassionate, giving, and sympathetic procurement agents the hospitals had ever dealt with. He really seemed to care.

The paramedics wheeled in the young motorcyclist on a blood-spattered gurney. The victim was motionless and his multi-colored helmet lay in two pieces between his bare feet. The face was unrecognizable, the skull split in the center of the forehead, what was left of a ruined brain protruding. ***You're fucked, bubba,*** Parkins thought gleefully. He noticed that the unfortunate young man was still being artificially respirated. ***Keep the goodies nice and fresh, guys.***

"Hello Mildred," Parkins dolefully acknowledged the aged admitting clerk.

"Hi, Mr. Parkins," she replied. "Looks bad. I'll let you know what's going on as soon as I know, okay? When the parents get here, too."

Parkins clasped Mildred's cold, clammy hands in his. "God bless you, Mildred. You're an angel."

After watching the brain-dead young man vanish into the emergency room, Parkins retired to the familiar green-pastel of the waiting room. He sat upright in a plastic chair, hands folded in his lap. His controlled breathing belied his excitement. He would never let his exuberance show in front of a victim's next of kin, though. The compassionate, helpful stranger was the appearance he had to convey. An act he had honed to near perfection. The number one procurement agent for Life Longevities was a role he took very seriously. Especially the money. And a score like this . . .

A wailing woman led by a pensive, hollow-eyed man entering the waiting room interrupted his avaricious revery. The parents. Andrew Parkins analyzed them quickly, accurately. Upper middle class, he surmised. They dressed smartly, even though they had done so in the numb hypnosis of blind panic. The woman was wearing a small gold crucifix. Excellent. Parkins studied his perfectly manicured fingertips in his lap as he listened to the woman's hysterics. Mildred tried to calm them.

"The doctor will let you know something as soon as possible," she said empathetically. "They are doing everything humanly possible for your son."

The man seemed to comprehend. He guided his shuddering, hiccuping wife to a chair, attempting fruitlessly to comfort her.

For the uncounted time, Parkins put himself in their place; it was his son dying, dead. He tasted the bitter agony, let his mind go dull with the unfathomable loss and inconsolable anguish. He found, curiously, that he rather enjoyed the morbid feeling. Mildred signaled him from the door, and like an imperceptible ghost, he faded from the waiting room.

"He's brain dead," Mildred whispered.

No shit, Parkins thought. ***His fucking brain was hanging out of his fucking skull, you stupid bitch.***

"I was afraid of that, Mildred," he said aloud.

"Doctor Michaels has him on artificial. They're blood typing now."

Parkins' mind was racing. "Organ donor card? Or listed on his driver's license?"

Mildred lowered her grey head shaking it slowly, solemnly.

Parkins grasped her shoulders lightly. "Thanks, Mildred. I'll take it from here."

Her rheumy green eyes glistened. "Good luck and Godspeed, Mr. Parkins."

Parkins moved quickly. From a hospital-provided computer terminal, he e-mailed the blood work to Slick Calisto, then found Doctor Arvid Michaels, a crusty old veteran of the emergency room wars. The old bastard was an obvious alcoholic, but one of the best E. R. men around.

"Damned shame," he remarked absently, stroking his salt and pepper beard. "Near perfect specimen. Serious damage mostly confined to the skull. All other applicable organs should be immaculate for harvest. Just need permission. You know the drill."

"Thanks, Doctor Michaels. Is the paperwork ready?"

"Yes, Mildred has all the necessary forms. I am going to speak to the parents now. Would you like to accompany me?"

Parkins nodded thoughtfully. "Could I have just a minute?"

Doctor Michaels grunted, smelling of Lavoris and Gilbey's. "Their son's not going anywhere at the moment."

Stepping outside, Parkins quickly dialed Slick's private number. He didn't wait for the salutation. "How do we look?"

"Grand slam, Parts. Fucking out of the park. We got tentative matches on ***everything.*** We can gut this motherfucker like a fish. Bring this one home, baby!" Slick was unusually excited.

"You just e-mail the hospital the destination information."

"You're gonna make us rich, you magnificent bastard!" Slick said, fingers clacking on a keyboard in the background.

"Rich***er***, my brother. Just remember who loves ya, Slick, and it ain't your momma!" Parkins disengaged the cell, removed the head set, stowing it inside his jacket. He primped his hair into place and walked back inside, the antiseptic smell of despair and death embracing him like an old friend.

Doctor Michaels met him at the entrance of the waiting room, handing him a sheaf of papers on a clipboard. "Ready?" the Doctor inquired.

Parkins nodded and the two strode through the doors.

Mr. and Mrs. Harlan E. Walters were informed that their son Jimmy had died as the result of severe head trauma sustained in a motorcycle accident at 1:40 a.m. The hospital staff did everything humanly possible to save the life of their son, but the damage was too serious to overcome. Jimmy was currently on an artificial respiration device, but there was no brain activity. Doctor Michaels introduced the grieving parents to Andrew Parkins of Life Longevity.

"I am terribly sorry," Michaels said sonorously. "Please listen to what Mr. Parkins has to say, Mr. and Mrs. Walters. I know it's difficult, but it is the right thing to do."

Mrs. Walters was, for all intents and purposes, ***gone.*** She sat bolt upright in her chair, pallor ghastly, respiration shallow, staring at some seemingly fixed point on the opposite wall.

Parkins knew he had to go for her, but ***through*** Mr. Walters.

"Sir? Harlan. May I call you Harlan?"

Walters nodded dumbly.

"Harlan, I know this is the most difficult time imaginable . . . but I would ask you to think of Jimmy's legacy. There is a great need out there, a need that Jimmy can help fulfill. Had Jimmy made his wishes known to you regarding organ donation?" Parkins spoke softly, and gave the words 'organ donation' a lilt that made it sound as though he were extolling the virtues of a new, improved denture cream.

Harlan Walters regarded his wife cautiously. Her mouth hung open and a thread of saliva drooled onto her sweater. "Uh, he never really said. I don't think I could bring myself to—"

"I understand completely, Harlan. I thought the same thing last year. My wife—" Parkins choked on a sob.

"My wife was killed by a drunk driver last year, Harlan. I thought the same thing as you. I couldn't bring myself to . . . to . . ." Parkins carefully wiped away an errant tear. "But Harlan, right now a 15-year-old girl, a 35-year-old father of five and a 19-year-old college athlete are alive today because of my wife. I like to think . . . I like to think she would have been proud of that." Parkins swallowed hard. He cautiously glanced at Mrs. Walters. So far, nothing was penetrating.

Mr. Walters shrugged. "I just don't know . . . "

Another tactic. A careful, probably untraceable lie. "Jimmy did indicate on his driver's license that he wished to be an organ donor."

Walters stared wide-eyed. "He did? I didn't know. Isn't that . . . automatic then?"

"No, sir. Many people think that. We still have to have written permission from the next of kin." Parkins lowered his head with mock humility.

"Well, I—"

"Sign it, Harlan," Mrs. Walters spoke up suddenly in a surprisingly strong, guttural voice. "If Jimmy wanted that, sign it."

"Evelyn, are—are you sure?"

She stared at him with blood-rimmed eyes. "Goddammit, sign the fucking papers, you spineless piece of shit!" she screamed venomously.

Harlan smiled bloodlessly. "Of course, dear. It'll be okay."

Of course, it wouldn't be. One week after Jimmy Walters was buried, Evelyn Walters placed her husband's Winchester 12-gauge shotgun beneath her chin, and pulled the trigger with the big toe of her right foot. It took Harlan nearly a year to drink himself to death after that.

Andrew "Parts" Parkins walked quietly down the hallways with the signed paperwork, barely suppressing the urge to dance. Within a few hours, Jimmy Walters' various organs were making their way to various points around the nation, via Fed Ex.

Slick was ecstatic and all but had phone sex with him. Tired, Parkins disconnected the line as he guided the BMW to his modest home in the suburbs just after dawn. All was quiet in the house. He checked in on little Travis, who was sleeping soundly. He softly kissed his son's forehead, which was slightly warm and clammy. Parkins stared thoughtfully at his son. Travis wouldn't have to grow up like he had, scared to death of everything and everyone, particularly his abusive father. Parkins would see to it that he was well-equipped to deal with life in general, and particularly the assholes of the world, whoever and wherever they might be. He would empower his son, mold him in the image of the adult Andrew Parkins—a man in control, not afraid, never allowing anyone or anything close enough to him to cause him pain. No fear, no guilt. No regrets, no contrition. Not a fucking doormat like he had once been.

Angela was sleeping restlessly in their bed. Dark smudges encircled her eyes. She had been quite plain when he married her, but he figured that would lessen the odds of her screwing around on him. She had been easy to dominate, almost too easy. A meek, mild, wounded bird kind of a woman. Parkins, who by then had become a master of manipulation, took total control of her within weeks of their first meeting. He needed someone to bear a child for him and she happened to be adequate for that need at the time. Now, he felt nothing much more than contempt for her.

Parkins grasped the sheet Angela was sleeping on, yanked it away, dumping her unceremoniously onto the floor. Panic-stricken, she screamed, awakening Travis, who began crying softly in the other room.

"Now look what you did, you stupid bitch," he spat, shoving her onto her back with his foot in the middle of her chest.

"I—I'm sorry," she stammered. "You scared me."

Parkins reached down, grasping Angela by the hair of the head. He yanked her to her feet with a painful yelp, and threw her across the bed into the opposite wall. She crumpled to the floor and began weeping softly.

"Get in there," Parkins said with studied calm, "and tend to our son. What did you end up doing last night?"

"Took him to the emergency room," Angela replied in a squeaky voice. "They got the fever down."

"Good. Now get in there." There was quiet menace in his voice.

"'Kay," she said, like a child. She excised a large circle across the room, around her husband. As she got to the door, Parkins raced over and kidney punched her. Angela doubled over and he grabbed her by the throat, straightening her up.

"Don't ever call me while I'm working," he whispered hotly into her ear. Parkins shoved his trembling wife into the hallway wall.

Parkins slept until nearly noon. Travis gurgling happily in the next room roused him. He slid into his robe and strolled into his son's room. He heard Angela very quietly rustling around downstairs, like the timid mouse she was. Parkins cupped his son's soft round, drool-coated chin.

"Won't be long, pal. It'll just be me and you." Parkins had heard those words before, in very nearly the same strange voice, a long time ago. A terrible vision replayed itself in his mind. He was riding in the 1963 Mercury Comet with his father, who had a Falstaff Beer in one hand, an unfiltered Chesterfield in the other. His dad put the beer between his legs and swatted his son—Andrew—hard across the face.

"Think fast!" he growled, after the fact. Andrew tasted coppery blood in his mouth and tried hard not to cry. "Too late, Shitbird!"

Parkins shook his head sharply to clear the waking nightmare. Travis eyed him curiously, then spit up on himself. He hadn't thought about dear old Dad for quite some time. ***How's the old pine box, Chief?*** Parkins thought. ***Bet the fucking worms are having a helluva time trying to eat you, you leathery old bastard.*** Parkins forced himself to smile at his son, swallowed hard, then took a long, scalding shower.

During the day, Parkins focused his efforts bartering for, and collecting fetuses from the abortion clinic across town. The demand (and the money) for research and development involving fetal tissue was phenomenal. Parkins had to hand it to Slick Calisto. Life Longevities was an abject anomaly in the usually chaste world of the OPO; the slimy night thing that had somehow slipped greasily through the moldy cracks. With uncanny administrative acumen, Calisto had managed to obtain (and maintain) the necessary Health Care Financing Administration certification as an OPO, and yet still, Slick seemed freely able to circumvent the system, extracting top dollar for organs and tissue at will. Even Life Longevities' Board of Directors consisting of top hospital officials, transplant surgeons and other professionals were unable to uncover the surreptitious financial operations. With Slick's extraordinary ability to navigate the labyrinth of Federal and state paperwork, perverting it to his own financial advantage, and Parts Parkins' acquisition skills, together they were nearly unstoppable.

Parkins fully planned to retire by fifty, in twelve years. He purposely lived modestly, with the exception of the one luxury he allowed himself—the BMW—and Angela was too frightened of him to attempt to spend his money, even if she could figure out where he had hidden it. As soon as Travis was a little closer to self-sufficiency, it was Parkins' intention to rid himself of his wife, one way or another. A wood-chipper would be his preferred method of choice, but in the interest of expediency, he figured he would just grab the kid and vanish, when the time came. Of course, he would always wonder if dismembering and disemboweling Angela would elicit some response from her quietly terrified demeanor.

The Motorola's chirp suspended his near-sexual fantasy. It was Slick.

"Thought I gave you the day off, Parts," His boss mock-scolded.

"I can rest when I die, Boss. On my way to Crosstown Clinic."

"Man, you got the hustle, I'll give you that."

"Hey, gotta get it while you can. The limeys already figured out how to clone transgenic lambs and pigs. Not too far away from preventing hyperacute rejection in xenotransplantation. Then, where we gonna be?"

Slick laughed. "You sound like a goddamn AMA Journal article. Life Longevities already has its little corporate fingers in the cloning pie. Animal, human, plant. Whatever it takes. If we need to clone headless human bodies to harvest, no problem. Hell, we buy fucking kids from Brazil or prisoners from China if that's what we need to do. There'll always be a way to make money—a ***lot*** of fucking money—if you look for it. That's why there'll always be a black market, Parts."

"Amen and hallelujah, brother," Parkins cracked.

"Go make us some of that cash, Parts."

"Hey, Slick. Know the difference between a truck load of bowling balls and a truckload of dead babies . . . ?"

"Yeah. About a quarter million dollars! Later, Parts."

Within minutes, Parkins pulled the BMW into a reserved parking space at the rear of the Crosstown Clinic, located in a shadowy, deteriorating edge of town. A lone, stooped old man with a long gnarled grey beard stood silent vigil in excess of the required fifty feet from the front of the place. He wore a sandwich board that read "Life is the only Choice." A garish full-color photo of a supposedly aborted fetus screamed from beneath the words. Parkins thought warmly of the dog he ran over the night before.

Doctor Wilfred Manners was yet another bent, wasted old man, albeit one with an unusual talent. Knotted, yellowed fingers clasped Parkins hand when he came in. Parkins smelled the nauseating stench of unbathed human flesh and tobacco. "How've you been, young man?" Manners asked.

"Fine, Doctor Manners, fine. And yourself?" Manners was one creepy old fuck, but one that performed the majority of the city's partial-birth abortions. A 'veritable abortin' machine', Slick had called him.

"Oh, can't complain. Right-to-lifers finally gave up on me, 'cept for that old homeless guy they posted out front. They give him drinkin' money to stand out there with that ridiculous sandwich board. He's not a bad sort. I give him a fifth once and again." Manners openly, absently rubbed his crotch.

"Great," Parkins beamed. "Do you have anything for Life Longevities today?"

Manners' pale pink tongue flitted between yellowed, crooked teeth and licked bloodless, liver-colored lips. "Yes. Oh, yes, indeed. Let me get you the charts." He smiled. "Got some nice ones lined up for you, son."

Parkins knew that he would. Life Longevities paid the rent on the property and owned the building where Crosstown Clinic was located. The Corporation also took care of all of Doctor Manners' employee expenses and even paid the electric bill. Last quarter, they paid off his condo.

Doctor Manners handed Parkins a clipboard and grinned proudly. Parkins flipped through the patient profiles and whistled softly. "Nice and clean, Doctor. No diseases, zero STD's, no genetic anomalies. I must say, I'm impressed. If I'm impressed, Life Longevities is impressed, too."

"Grand, Mr. Parkins. Shall we get started?"

"Proceed, Maestro," Parkins smiled.

Doctor Manners performed thirteen partial-birth abortions in six and a half hours. Parkins packed organ groups, cardiac blood, cell samples, a small package of eyeballs and even whole fetuses into dry ice-lined coolers and had them Fed Ex'd, UPS'd or couriered to various universities, tissue researchers, or pharmaceutical companies as had been previously requisitioned. Shortly after dark, Manners returned to the back office.

Parkins grinned at him. "Problem, Doctor?"

Manners nodded tiredly. He scratched his forehead absently, leaving a dark red smudge from a bloodied latex glove. "The last girl . . . second thoughts. I was thinking that you could . . ."

"Say no more, Doctor." ***My specialty***, Parkins thought.

Gina Ridgemont was seventeen, still in high school, unmarried and scared to death.

Parkins bestowed upon her his most expansive, paternal, knowing, sympathetic smile.

"Hello, Gina," he said, concerned but amiable. "I'm Andrew Parkins. I'm a minister. Perhaps I could be of some help here."

She was emaciated, her pasty face pocked-marked with violent reddish-purple acne. Her mousy brown hair hung limp and lifeless, framing her puffy, swollen face. Tears streamed from her eyes, mucous from her nose onto her lips. "I—I'm afraid," she whimpered.

Think of the poor bastard who knocked you up, Jesus Christ!

"Listen, Gina. There's absolutely nothing to be afraid of. Doctor Manners has done this many, many times. And you aren't the only girl who's found herself in this situation. Believe me, God understands what you are about to do. What you ***need*** to do."

She hiccupped, blowing a wad of snot across the room. "But, shouldn't I just go ahead and have it . . . then let someone adopt it?"

Parkins drew a deep breath. All bets would've been off had the snot ball found its way onto his suit. He winced inwardly and took her pallid, clammy hand. "Look inside yourself, Gina. You know yourself, what's right for you. You have to do what's best for you. Because in the end, that's what will be best for everyone in the long run. Do you understand?"

It hadn't been the words so much as the hypnotic tone in which Parkins spoke them. The words caressed her, wound their way inside her head, calmed her guilty soul. She reminded Parkins of Angela—easily manipulated—so very easily.

Gina's glistening eyes locked with his. "Thank you, Father. I'm ready. I'll go back, now."

Parkins nodded solemnly, biting the inside of his cheek to keep from laughing. He made the sign of the cross—backwards—and she lowered her head as if in absolution. "Go with God, my child. He forgives all."

She nodded, and disappeared through the worn doorway. Parkins regarded himself in the empty lobby's mirror. A small grin played at one corner of his mouth. ***Cha-Ching! Yessssss! Once more, victory snatched from the jaws of defeat.***

After the last shipment was made, Parkins made his way home, after Slick assured him that he would give him a call if anything good was working. He ate Angela's bland cooking with hungry gusto, played happily with his giggling young son, and totally ignored his weary wife, who also purposefully avoided any contact with her husband.

Parkins slept restlessly that night, plagued by not-quite-nightmares that slipped in and out of his mind tauntingly like amorphous shadows. They were dreams he would not be able to remember later in much detail. More of a depressing, morbid feeling, a virulent contagion of angst-ridden emotion. He could recall seeing his father fleetingly, as he might appear now, some twelve years after his death. Most of the flesh had melted (been eaten?) away, only some of his cancer-ridden internal organs remained, entangled by leathery sinew within the yellow-gray rib cage. But the skeletal remains somehow managed to convey perfectly the swaggering demeanor of his late father. Even the grinning skull seemed to smirk arrogantly. The dreams, like his father, faded torpidly back into the earth, muffled distant screaming finally echoing into nothingness, claimed by the slow passage of time. "Think fast," the raspy voice said abruptly in his head, just before he awoke.

Everything seemed ashen and grey that morning. Even Travis was not his usual ebullient self. Angela, conversely enough, didn't seem quite as dreary as she normally appeared. For the first time since he was a child, Parkins felt out of place, inadequate, almost hopelessly lost. Calisto was uncharacteristically incommunicado; his much younger wife answered the phone after a few dozen tries and countless rings, announcing that she "didn't know where the fuck that bastard Slick was and didn't much give a damn," before unceremoniously—and rather loudly—hanging up.

Even the BMW felt strange to him. Parkins sat forlornly in the E. R. parking lot of Good Hope. He watched with detachment as the ambulances brought their crushed, broken, bleeding charges to hopeful salvation. He thought of the hundreds of human organ deals he had brokered. He thought of the pain, suffering and anguish that were the ancillary by-products of his stock-in-trade. Parkins felt like he wanted to care, but seemed unable to elevate himself to that plateau.

Finally, the cell trilled away the quiet.

"Hello?" Parkins asked timidly, in someone else's voice.

There was a sharp staccato burst, then a nearly unintelligible murmur. Parkins ripped the headset from his skull and threw it to the floor. He was sure—he knew—what had been said. He just wasn't sure who could have said it.

"Think fast."

A rattled Andrew Parkins returned home, after another attempt at contacting Slick Calisto. A smarmy, yuppie-type voice informed Parkins that Mr. Calisto was "unavoidably indisposed at the time," could he take a message? Parkins hung up.

The Parkins home was cold, dark and empty. Almost. Parkins found the front door standing wide open as he wheeled the BMW into the drive. He dashed into the house, calling for Angela. No answer, save the mocking reverberation of his own exigent voice. He smelled something musky vaguely masking something ***rotted*** hanging in the still, stale air. Parkins felt ice dance up his spine when he heard—

—a small gurgling—

—upstairs, where it naturally should have been. Travis' room.

Parkins took the steps three at a time heading upstairs, in his sheer terrified panic not noticing, although nearly slipping in the bloody footprints smeared into the carpeted steps.

He flung open the door to the nursery, concern overcoming his gripping terror. Travis was sitting in his basinet, grinning and waving his chubby arms animatedly. The sign of relief hitched in Parkins' throat when he saw . . .

A thin ribbon of red had been traced across the breadth of Travis' forehead, just above the brow. Another etched the length of Travis' torso, in a Y-shape. Parkins knew what it was supposed to represent—the delineations used by the coroner at an autopsy.

It took every fiber of Parkins' being not to run. His eyes finally found the bloody footprints seeping into the ochre carpet. They paused in front of the basinet, then strolled casually across the room, disappearing beneath the closet door.

Parkins crept cautiously into the room, straining to hear the slightest creak of the closet door, the rattle of the doorknob, the telltale squeak of a protesting hinge. Four steps to Travis, just four. If Angela had been killed already, too fucking bad. No one was taking Travis, no one.

The stench of disease, blood and putrefaction was overwhelming. Parkins choked back the font of vomit staging itself at the base of his esophagus and gathered up his son. Just as he was turning to run from the room, a sticky, wet hand clamped onto his forearm. Travis squirmed from his grasp and tumbled back into the basinet with a surprised gasp.

Parkins' urinated himself and his bowels let go. Some faraway rational remnant of him figured that those autonomic reactions were the precursors to his death, but he was still alive, still breathing in that insanely controlled way he had. What had him by the forearm was impossible; nothing like what Andrew "Parts" Parkins was looking at could possibly exist.

It was an oozing, shambling wreck of a being, in roughly human format. It resembled an adult human male for the most part, except that it appeared to have been turned ***inside out.*** As if something were trying to escape from within, the torso swelled and writhed in unlikely places. Unfortunately analytical in spite of being in a giddy state of shock, Parkins could clearly see pulsing veins and arteries snaking across the surface of the inverted, blood-slicked skin. Some of the more recognizable organs protruded externally, near where they would normally have been encased within. A mishapened heart beat slowly on the outside of the rib cage, intestines squirmed and groaned tiredly on the exterior of the thing's groin. It peered at him through white eyeballs, the vague shadow of the irises gazing from somewhere inside the darkened sockets. The face split into something like a smile, too-white, perfect teeth appearing behind a curtain of fleshy lips turned inside out. Parkins abruptly recognized the face.

Slick Calisto.

But the height of the thing was all wrong for Calisto. It was leaner, as well, and one arm was muscular, the other flaccid, flabby. It staggered as if one leg were shorter than the other. The hand's grip was like a vise; dark blood flowed across Parkins' arm from the thing's oozing hand, murky water from a sodden sponge.

"What—what do you want?" Parkins asked in a hushed, tremulous whisper, once he found his voice.

"What would you give up, to save your own life?" The thing answered a question with a question. The voice was a fluid, multi-layered chorus; what appeared to be Calisto's mouth lay slack and dead. It was coming from somewhere deep within.

"I don't understand . . . " Parkins replied meekly, barely controlling the impulse to scream.

The dead fish-mouth curved upward at the corners. Something else was pulling those strings. "It's a simple enough question. How important is your life to you?"

Parkins' hand was going numb; he could feel the bones in his arm grinding together. "I would do anything to stay alive," he whispered, naked before the thing.

With the other, more muscular arm, the entity scooped a giggling Travis up, nestling the child to its breast. The perverse smile widened, an exploded black tongue flicked the child's head.

"Noooooo—" Parkins keened pitifully.

"You said ***anything,***" the voices rejoined cheerfully. "It's your choice. You or the boy." The hand released him and Parkins sank to the floor, sobbing harshly.

"No, not my son . . . not Travis," he wept. Parkins saw a shape float to the surface of the exposed sinew of the thing's expansive thigh. It was a fetus, wriggling beneath. "God, no . . . "

"God will understand," the chorus sang. "God forgives all."

"It's a simple choice," Parkins heard his own voice say.

"I want to ***live.*** I fucking want to live. There, I said it. Take the boy, not me. God. Please, don't let this happen to me." Parkins vomited convulsively onto the carpet.

Parkins shrieked and crawled on his hands and knees out of the room. He blindly tumbled down the carpeted stairs and came to rest in a heap on the landing. He faded out of consciousness for a few moments, and when he came to, the thing was standing over him, staring at him with pale, backwards eyes. The powerful arms lifted Parkins from the floor, bringing him to eye level with the composite from Hell. Parkins smelled the overpowering stink of sickness, decay, bile—and surprisingly, Old Spice—emanating from that horror of horrors.

"But you said—" Parts Parkins stammered.

"God will understand," the voices rang out.

The entity pulled Parkins closer and closer, finishing in a forceful bear hug. Parkins felt himself sinking inside the thing, tiny hands clutching at him, drawing him irrevocably inside. Calisto's mouth opened impossibly wide to consume Parkins' entire head. And then Parkins was gone.

There is a threshold of pain that the human psyche simply cannot withstand; it mercifully shuts down the works, beginning with consciousness. Parkins faded in and out, dancing precariously along the razor's edge of toleration and oblivion. In the wake of the relentlessly mind-searing pain, he could feel he was being consumed—from within.

The ambulance had taken him to Good Hope. All the technology known to man had been employed to keep what was left of him alive. Doctor Deborah Temple, a devout, hopeful woman as well as a highly skilled physician, had never seen such a quickly devastating, wide-spread assault on a previously healthy human being. Practically every organ in Andrew Parkins' body was stricken with some disease or the other. That was the other bizarre thing—blood analysis and biopsies detected at least fifteen different kinds of maladies. Unheard of.

The murk was not so thick that Parkins was unaware of what was going on around him. Doctor Temple and Angela were in the room with him.

"Perhaps we should discuss this outside," Doctor Temple cautioned quietly.

Angela's soft voice spoke with determination. "No, Doctor. If there's even a remote chance he can hear us, I want him to know what we are doing for him. How we are going to help him."

The doctor sighed. "Very well. Prognosis is extremely poor. Six types of cancer are present in nearly every major organ. He has developed cataracts, advanced cirrhosis of the liver, bone marrow disease and there are malignant tumors in his brain. He is being kept alive via a respirator. That he is alive at all is a minor miracle."

"There's nothing you can do?" The meek voice of his wife asked.

"We can keep him alive for as long as his body will continue to function in spite of the diseases."

"How long?"

"Several months, I would guess. But, I think you should seriously consider termination of—"

"No, Doctor. Andrew always said he believed where there's life, there's hope."

Parkins attempted to interject, but found he could not.

"Keep him alive for as long as is possible," Angela said pointedly. And then with a slight lilt, "and money's not an issue. There's plenty."

"Very well, Mrs. Parkins. We'll abide by your wishes." The Doctor sounded doubtful.

“Thank you, you’ve been wonderful. Please let me know if there’s any change. I have to go home now and tend to my son. He’s with my mother.”

Noooooooooo!

Parkins felt the pervasive corruption within, as well as the infestation of tubes, wires, catheters and apparatus snaking throughout his body. He wanted—needed—to scream, but couldn’t. He found—eventually—that the ever-present, searing, blinding agony was able to scream for him, shrieking inside his skull until his diseased mind was raw and bleeding.

The Calling by Paul Melniczek

Ocean waves pounded the craggy rocks far below, the white foam spilling over the jagged shoreline. Tiny mussels and sea crustaceans covered the massive boulders that served as first defense against the relentless onslaught of the timeless surf.

Mitch Richards gazed down and felt a pang of sadness, knowing that his brief trip to the quaint little town was nearly at an end.

Griever's Bluff had been quite a find for the magazine journalist. Coincidence more than anything else had led him to the sleepy New England village.

While out for a drink with several of his fellow workers, he had been referred to the Sea Whisper Bed and Breakfast by Mark Adams, one of the marketing reps at the publication.

Mark was well known for advice on inns and restaurants of the Eastern shore resorts, and when Mitch had mentioned a week away from home with peace and rest foremost in mind, the salesman told him he knew a great place, secluded and off the map.

The autumn air was brisk and fresh, teasing Mitch's skin with a taste of the winter season that was soon to arrive. He pulled his sweatshirt tighter and admired the fantastic view which could not be captured in any description or portrait.

Gripping the metal support rail, his eyes traced the bottom of the steep cliff directly below where he stood, then moved north to the modest wooden boat dock that served the local fishermen.

The town was nestled in a wooded cove, the houses set on a gradual incline leading to the water's edge where tall cliffs loomed on either side.

Mitch had walked around the cobblestone streets and mingled with the pleasant inhabitants throughout his stay at the bed and breakfast. There were few visitors during the year and although genuinely friendly, Mitch thought that they probably preferred it that way.

He couldn't blame them.

It was growing late and Mitch wondered where Mary Gail was, the widowed owner of the inn.

She had gone away yesterday after finding out that her cousin had fallen gravely ill.

Mary had apologized but Mitch fully understood her predicament. He was leaving Friday anyway. One day alone at the place was not a problem, so she left her guest to provide for himself. The kitchen was stocked and Mitch was permitted to have the run of the place for his last two days there, but Mary said she would return Friday morning at latest to see him off.

The woman had played the perfect host all week, and actually only rented rooms to referrals. Mitch was paid up until Friday, and originally had intended to stay for two weekends.

Mary had stated flat out that it would be impossible, and emphasized rather strongly that Mitch had to leave before Saturday, and her place was the town's only inn.

That conversation had seemed a trifle odd at the time and Mitch had put it out of mind. He recalled it clearly now as he looked down the road leading to the front entrance.

He started towards the house, deciding to spend the evening reading a novel and sipping the sweet wine that was in ample supply. The other night he had gone to the Red Tavern, a small pub catering to thirsty locals, but he didn't feel like driving down to town.

Mitch smiled with envy as he took a last glance at the majestic ocean, wishing he could take a piece of the town's magic back home to New York with him.

Mary Gail felt the need for urgency as she drove her sedan up the heavily forested road. It was already dusk and she had over a two hour drive left to return home.

She liked Mitch and had enjoyed his company the past several days. Sometimes it grew lonely at the house. She really didn't mind keeping up the place but had few tenants in the fall anyway.

October wasn't the time for having visitors. Especially near the end of the month, as it was now.

She would have said no, but the money flow had been light as of late.

Well, as long as he was gone by tomorrow everything would be fine.

Mary shuddered at the thought of the upcoming weekend.

Friday was All Soul's Eve.

Had it been a full year already?

Taking a deep breath, Mary tried to calm her nerves.

A wandering mind can lead to distraction, she thought to herself. Pay attention to the highway.

As if in answer to that lingering thought, a large deer erupted from the bushes scant yards in front of Mary's car, springing onto the road without hesitation.

She made a desperate attempt to avoid striking the animal, but there was not enough time or room to spare.

With a sickening thud, the helpless creature was struck head on by the vehicle and knocked a dozen yards to the side.

A short scream broke from the woman's lips as she veered off the road and crashed into a sprawling acorn tree, the tiny nuts dropping down on the mangled hood of the car like angry hailstones from the heavens

Mary Gail slumped over the steering wheel, motionless and battered.

Drops of blood poured forth from an ugly cut on her forehead as a result of colliding with the now shattered windshield glass.

The woods were silent except for the mournful cry of an owl in the distance as it roused for the night's hunt.

Golden rays of morning sunlight greeted the waking face of Mitch, promising the start of a gorgeous day.

He yawned deeply, scratching his tousled brown hair and stretching lean arms behind his soft pillow.

Rolling over, Mitch looked at his alarm clock which he had forgotten to set. It was almost eleven.

Had he overslept that late?

So engrossed was he in the book last night, the hours had flown by with little regard to the time. Several glasses of the wine didn't help matters either.

Where was Mary Gail at, Mitch again wondered? Check out time was now past, and still he had slumbered undisturbed. Maybe she was making up for her hasty departure by letting him rest. He would just have to wait for that answer until he talked to her, he thought.

What a day to sleep in late, the thirty year old mused to himself. Birds were outside whistling in shrill pitches, and the early frost was fading from the window pane.

He was tired yet, and had a slight headache. That was definitely from the wine.

Reluctantly, Mitch raised himself up and headed for the shower.

It would be a long drive back, but he was looking forward to throwing his efforts into work again. His stay here had been refreshing, but he felt a sudden urge to leave the little town for the first time since arriving.

Probably a bit of home sickness, he thought. That's all.

But the feeling stayed with him, and did not go away.

After preparing and eating a late breakfast by himself, Mitch had taken down his luggage and loaded everything in his small sports coupe.

Realizing that it would be rude to simply write a thank-you note and drive off, he made the best of his situation and strolled leisurely about the grounds of the inn, taking in the vitality and color.

Many of the leaves had fallen already, but there remained some spots of orange and yellow in the lofty boughs. Mary Gail kept her property trimmed and clean, with great attention to detail.

The wooden porch which fronted the house was decorated in the traditional harvest style. Pumpkins were carefully laid out and Indian Corn was hanging from the exposed beams covering the porch ceiling, which was complete with a bench, sitting chairs, and a hammock which swung lazily in the sea breeze.

Here Mitch sat down and looked at his watch. It was going on two and Mary Gail was nowhere to be seen. What had happened to her, he thought? Maybe her cousin was not doing too well and she was forced to stay longer.

Sighing, the journalist rubbed his clean shaven face and began to feel uneasy.

He had been tense ever since waking, and couldn't seem to shake it all day. Mitch blamed it on returning to work soon and most likely the long drive back. Some of his trepidation was concern over the whereabouts of the innkeeper, he admitted.

She was a feisty but kind lady, and had a mundane work ethic that was rooted in the old customs of the countryside she lived in. It could not have been easy taking care of the place by herself. Mary Gail was nearing sixty, but looked and acted a decade less.

Mitch would be uncomfortable if he left without seeing her, but he felt equally about remaining there after her insistence that he leave by Friday morning at latest.

For whatever reason, that conversation played in his mind and abruptly he stood.

The right thing to do would be to leave her a polite note, and call at a later time.

Mitch went into the house and found a scratch pad. Brief but to the point, he finished a letter of thanks and placed it on the kitchen table.

He looked wistfully at the inn one last time then entered his car.

Turning the ignition key, he was greeted by a dull click as the engine refused to turn over.

Mitch bit his tongue before any choice words could come out, and folded his arms.

It appeared he wasn't going anywhere at the moment.

Pain flooded through the body of Mary Gail.

Every part of her felt bruised and she drifted in and out of dreams filled with anguish and darkness.

The same nightmare closed in our subconscious mind. A feeling of growing dread permeated her senses, and of time running out.

She had suffered a bad head wound and was laying in the critical ward at Blue Oaks Hospital.

When a police officer had found the stricken woman, he didn't hesitate in taking her directly for help. To wait for an ambulance would have cost Mary Gail her life. She was on the ground and the car had been in danger of catching on fire.

The officer thought only to rescue the victim and in his haste had left the woman's purse with her identification at the scene.

Slightly conscious when she was discovered, her bloodied lips rasped out a dire warning to the officer who listened in horror to what he heard.

"Leave, the damned ones come...................................."

Mitch sat on the ground next to his car, picking up a stone and tossing it into some nearby bushes.

Frustrated and angry, he regretted his decision to stay and try getting his car running.

He had a decent working knowledge of engine mechanics, but had failed at every attempt known to him in starting his coupe.

"Not the battery, not the alternator, not the wires, not the fuel pump," he grumbled.

"I give up."

The journalist was mentally and physically drained. His hands and shirt were filthy, and he was at his wit's end.

If he had walked for help earlier, one of the local garages would probably have had him up and running by now. It was a good two or more miles to town, and his unwillingness to go on foot had won out over fixing the car himself.

He worked without pause the entire afternoon, and there was nothing to show for his efforts.

The day had come and gone quickly, due in part to his late stay in bed.

Sunset was fading and the air had swiftly grown colder.

Mitch went into the house hoping to reach the garage for some assistance.

He found the small local directory and dialed the number for two auto shops in town. At both places the phone rang without an answer.

"That's strange, I guess they're all done for the day." He shook his head and knew that his stay was to be extended an additional night anyway.

The owner remained unaccounted for and Mitch went to his room to wash off the residue of his fruitless exertions. After cleaning up he cooked himself some of the oyster stew that Mary Gail made earlier in the week.

Mitch sat at the kitchen table for a while and then walked out to the back deck with its view of the ocean below.

The night was cloudless.

A full moon shone brightly overhead, and the waters moved in brimming waves, answering to the ageless pull of gravity. Besides the crashing of the sea, there were other noises that the journalist had become accustomed to hearing. The fall insects, crickets chirping in their calming tones.

Tonight there was only silence.

For the first time all week, Mitch felt like a stranger to the receptive sea village.

The sense of anxiety he woke up with had increased all day and now spread further into his wandering thoughts.

He wished that Mary Gail would pull up the lane, and at least reassure him that all was well, but the roads were empty and silent.

The whole night seemed watchful and restless, and Mitch could feel the tension around him.

It was unnatural.

He returned into the house and made his way to the living area, which served as a great spot to relax and read. Earlier he had retrieved the novel from the packed luggage and resumed his story, so he sat down and found his bookmark.

Mitch propped his feet on a cushioned stool and sat back. If nothing else the pursuit would be a distraction from the odd feeling that weighed on him.

The words lost meaning as weary eyes grew heavy. The journalist had to repeat several paragraphs when he lost his place, and the sentences blended together as he closed his eyes for longer intervals with every blink.

Mitch awakened from sleep, the dream lingering for a brief moment then lost forever.

The room had grown cold, and the curtain to one of the windows swayed in the night ocean breeze. In that fragile period of light awareness, the sound of a distant bell reached Mitch's hearing.

He reached full alertness and squinted his eyes, peering into the darkness outside.

Had he imagined the sound? Bells?

Glancing at his watch, he was surprised to see that it was now just past midnight.

Standing, his back was stiff from sleeping in the chair.

He went to the window and stuck his head out.

There was the strong smell of salt in the air. More powerful than what he recalled earlier.

Again, he heard the sound of a bell being tolled.

Yes, there was no mistaking it now.

A solemn ringing in the night, coming from the town.

Mitch grabbed his jacket and went to the front porch. He was curious as to why a bell would be ringing in the dead of night.

The wind blew through his hair, chill and biting. The sound had ceased, but he was convinced that what he heard was a bell. Maybe from the old church in the town square.

But why at midnight?

On All Hallows Eve of all times?

Maybe a local custom? He was not familiar with this being done elsewhere, but it was certainly possible.

A sudden disturbing thought then struck him, instantly clenching around his heart.

What if something had happened to Mary Gail?

Was this a way to inform the townspeople of dire news? An alarm of sorts?

The idea made Mitch cold, and the isolation of the inn closed about him. He didn't like his present circumstance, and needed to take some action.

Any action.

But what could he do?

The bell sounded again and Mitch shivered.

Whatever was going on, he wanted to find answers. And the only way was to walk to town.

Not wishing to go off in the night unprepared, he went back inside and grabbed an oil lamp with a thin metal handle. He lit the wick and went outside again, walking down the lane.

Stars glittered in the clear sky and the journalist could see his breath in the smoky light from the lamp.

The road was bordered by a dark forest of mixed hardwood and pine trees.

He seemed to be the only living creature in the world. Nothing stirred. The shadows crept up to his light and seemed to covet the scant radiance it gave off.

Mitch told himself that it was only the strange surroundings but the anxiety remained.

The bell tolled in the town below and Mitch continued like a forsaken will-o-the-wisp wandering eternally in the night.

The minutes dragged on and he strained his ears for any other significant sound but there was none. The road curved ahead and he knew that he was nearing the dock area as it swung about leading towards the center of town.

Several stone houses were within sight and he felt a slight sense of relief which vanished after he realized that they were enmeshed in total darkness.

Not a single light or candle was visible. This was very disquieting.

Throughout the valley rang the bell. The only sound beside his own breathing.

Mitch passed the homes and his hopes dwindled at the lonely sight. Was this normal in the area not to leave any lights on? Mary Gail certainly did—every night. Again he thought of the woman and he ground his teeth together. Was she all right?

The sound of the surf became noticeable and he was nearing the ocean. Mitch had been down at the dock earlier in the week and it was a busy but cheerful place. The pier guardhouse loomed up ahead and he could make out the outlines of the small fishing boats at dock.

Not a shred of light broke from the shadowed wharf.

Mitch thought it strange that the beam at the roof of the guardhouse was not even lit up for ships at sea. This could not be the practice. It was unsafe to say the least.

As he faced the sea, the bell continued to ring. It would sound for a few seconds, then pause. There seemed to be a mysterious repetition to it, a pattern or signal, but to what purpose he was confounded.

The journalist turned inland again and was not too far from the main part of town. He had taken only a couple of steps when a new sound rang in the night.

Another bell.

But this one came from the ocean.

It was answering the church bell.

Mitch gazed passed the dock and was astonished at what he saw.

A small ship was floating into port. There had been nothing on the water only seconds ago.

Yet here it approached.

The moonlight shone down on the vessel and Mitch gasped in horror.

A mist shimmered around the boat but did not appear elsewhere. And inside the shrouded fog the boat radiated with an unholy dim glow.

The inland bell rang and the boat responded to the call. It had docked and now Mitch could see forms appearing on the pier.

Sailors returning from sea. His eyes grew wide.

They were transparent.

Spectral figures moving slowly towards land. And him as well.

Mitch stood transfixed in utter terror.

He knew that something incredible was taking place and he was an unwelcome visitor. Mitch stumbled backwards and ran down the road towards town.

Not daring to look behind him, the journalist passed the homes and work places of the inner village. All was dark and locked.

This night belonged to the dead.

The sound of the bells continued and Mitch saw the church steeple in the distance, the source of the first bell. He headed towards it with his only thought to reach safety and worry about explanations later. Someone had to be ringing that bell.

Expecting to find the church doors locked and bolted, Mitch saw them thrown open wide and he leaped up the stone stairway that served as the entrance.

He entered the building and stopped.

Candles were lit on every table and shelf.

Lurid shadows danced on the walls, cast off from the numerous flames.

The bell rang from the altar and Mitch slowly walked on.

As he drew near he could see someone standing alone, hands resting on the rope. It was the minister.

"Reverend, what in heaven's name is going on?" Mitch approached the man who had not seen him arrive.

The minister gasped aloud as Mitch startled him. "What are you doing out! Do you know what night this is?"

"No. I am visiting the town. At Mary Gail's place. I've seen spirits at the dock!"

"You are a stranger then," the minister replied. "You were not meant to be here." He sighed. "Come up with me quick. The dead draw near."

Mitch hurried forward and stood with the minister who again tugged at the bell rope.

"They approach for repentance. Cursed as the consequence for their treacherous deeds. They are the crew of the ship *Dalion.* This is the night that they answer the summons, asking for forgiveness. Betrayed their friends to the British almost two hundred years ago. Traitors to the town and humanity."

A growing dread clutched Mitch's heart as he looked down the church for the entrance of the ghostly crew. Far off he heard the bell ringing from the dock.

The minister picked up a bible from the altar, holding the cross around his neck tightly.

"Destined to walk the streets on the night of all souls, they answer the calling every year. This has been going on for almost two centuries, and they appear in the church. Their reward from the British was a hangman's noose, a worthy prize for turning in their patriotic kinsmen. I can only pray for them. I have not the power to end their journey."

An eerie glow materialized from the church doorway and the damned crew entered.

A host of figures came forward and Mitch was frozen with dread.

The minister was terrified but he held his ground, whispering a prayer as they approached.

Mitch could see through them and his mouth gaped in revulsion at their ghastly faces.

His worst nightmare could not have envisioned a more desolate and horrid company of horrors. The faces were without hope and held a hunger for a release from their fate.

The minister held the good book high and his voice shook with the strain placed upon his office.

"You have answered the calling, and I pray for your forgiveness. Many have suffered from your heinous crimes against your fellow man and you suffer the fate. May you find the rest you seek."

He made a sign of benediction and the spirits paused for several endless moments, then slowly turned around, drifting back into the church.

Mitch's chest felt constricted at the unbelievable scene and he was drenched in a cold sweat.

He leaned on the minister for support as the lonely crew disappeared from sight and would have collapsed to the floor if the minister had not held him up.

The journalist didn't speak again that night as the minister took him down into the church basement where he spent the rest of the night and early morning in a tormented sleep without peace.

The minister received word the next day as to the condition of Mary Gail.

She was seriously hurt but would survive, although the full extent of her injuries was yet to be determined. Mentally, she seemed to be extremely distraught, and the minister understood why.

Mitch said little the next day as the garage worked on getting his car running again. His new host arranged to pay for the fees and Mitch could only mumble a quiet "Thank you."

Later on that afternoon he departed from the town of Griever's Bluff never to return.

He carried with him nightmares and a haunted look deep within his eyes that only someone with a very keen mind could see.

Angel Killer by Horns

"The Mind is the great Slayer of the Real" - Madame Blavatsky

"I thought that they were angels, but to my surprise . . . " - Styx, 'Come Sail Away'

Nightclub: The Rage.
Location: Cincinnati, Ohio.
Time: 02:45 AM

The ragged-looking stranger scowled over the crowd, searching for something or someone. His dark eyes studying everything around him like a hawk. Omen, tired and confused, sat across from him watching and waiting for him to say something. Only minutes before, they had escaped death. The stranger had saved his life, but from what he couldn't explain. Omen noticed a small scar over the stranger's right eyebrow. He could see that the clothes the man wore hadn't been cleaned in a long time, leather and cotton, every article baggy. Underneath them he was harboring a mobile arsenal of weapons. Omen had seen a few of them when they were attacked. He was thirsty and sweaty, but more than that he was in dire need of answers.

"We're okay for now," the stranger said, looking over at the kid who had just almost gotten his head mashed into *hamburger-helper*.

"What in the hell was it?" Omen asked, while sitting up in the black vinyl seat, placing his forearms on the table, and leaning forward. A look of puzzlement glowing in his eyes was as intense as the nightclub's neon sign.

"An angel . . . a fucking divine spirit! You know, those saintly messenger's of God, those winged son's of bitches you learned about in Sunday school when you were a boy. Right! The creatures that watch over 'us' as guardians because . . . that's the question right there. Because why? That thing wasn't watching over you, was it! No, I think we both know what it was trying to do."

"An angel," Omen said, shaking his head in ridicule. "You must be crazy!" He slapped both hands down on the table and began bursting with laughter. The impact caused a plastic salt shaker to roll off onto the floor. The stranger gave him an incensed stare.

"Yeah, that's real fucking funny, isn't it? We'll see if you're still laughing when they find you again," the stranger said with contempt, and then stood up and started to leave.

"Wait, I'm sorry. I need to know what's going on," Omen said, quickly changing his attitude. He couldn't deny what he had seen and what they had fought against. He wished he'd been tripping on something at the time, but he knew he was clean. There was nothing he could do to convince himself that it hadn't happened. This guy knew something, and he had to have some kind of an explanation, even if it was whacked.

The stranger halted and looked him over. Omen studied his appearance a little more closely this time. The guy was athletically built, broad-shouldered and strong. He had a blond-goatee that matched the color of his shoulder-length curly hair. Omen thought that the dude was cool, kind of in a *Kurt Russell "Escape from New York"* way. He had that kind of deep smooth voice that made you take him seriously. The stranger sat back down.

"I don't have *all* the answers, and never probably will . . . but I'm learning, and they know it."

There was a sudden explosion! Omen jumped back, and saw the stranger reach inside of his red-leather coat. At almost the same time, they both realized that it was a sound effect. The crowd cheered and danced beneath raining silver confetti streamers. The techno-mix of *Marilyn Manson's "Dope Hat"* and the pulsating colored lights, raged on.

"Fucking dance clubs," the stranger said as he relaxed. "So what's your name?"

"Everyone calls me Omen . . . because of the movies. I don't know, I guess because I can be as mean as *'Damien'* the anti-Christ," he said, and snickered. The stranger just looked at him, giving no expression.

"You're going to have to be when it comes time to fight them."

"So what you killed was an angel? That's hard too swallow . . . I'm sorry but it is."

"What they really are, I couldn't tell you. I just know that "Angels" are what we humans call them. It's the name they've given us. They've given us everything around us . . . they've given us a lie! They cultivate us like fucking cattle, we're slaves in their fucking prison!" He stopped talking and could tell that the kid wasn't following him. Sometimes I guess I can let my emotions get away from me, he thought to himself.

"But angels? I thought angels were servants to God, I thought they helped us?"

"That's what they want mankind to think. They like it even better when someone doesn't believe in them. But what they hate is when one of us can see them . . . oh, that really pisses them off!" He pointed to the scar above his eyebrow. It wasn't very big, but it was deep. It had that purplish-color that indicated that something had penetrated far below the skin.

"Wow, this shit is fucked!" Omen said, and then rested his back against the seat. "I really don't understand. Tell it to me like a story, you know, like . . . *In the beginning* . . ." The stranger halfway smiled. It was the first time he had seen the guy smile, and it made him smile. It made the stranger seem more human, Omen thought.

"Okay, I don't know when the beginning was, or what that would even mean, but I don't believe that humans originated here. Here in this reality, that is to say. I tend to think that we were brought here and bred here."

Omen stopped him, saying, "So angels brought us here? Is that what you mean?"

"Well, yes and no. These creatures, beings that we call angels, aren't from our dimension, that I'm sure of. See, once you under-stand that reality is changeable, that other dimensions exist . . . then you'll start to comprehend things. You've already seen, and you'll see more. You're a 'Seer', you have many talents, and you'll begin to discover them and get them down . . . in time. And in the process, you'll learn how physically demanding they can be. Reality is a big thing to toy with." He reached forward with one hand, holding it open, palm up. "Give me your hand."

"Which one?" Omen asked, alarmed.

"It doesn't matter, they're both the same," the stranger said, and looked at his own outstretched one.

Omen hesitantly moved his right hand toward him.

"Relax, I'm going to give it back," the stranger said, and grabbed him by the wrist, turning his hand to where the palm could be seen. "Look at the lines in your hand . . . you see them?"

Omen focused on his palm, but it was difficult to see in the blinking lights of the club. He realized that he had never looked at the lines, or at least couldn't remember ever doing so.

"In the occult, these lines can tell a great deal about a person. There's your heart line, your head line, your life line, and your fate line. You see?" He looked up at Omen, waiting for an answer.

After a few moments he said, "Yes, I think I found them all, but . . ."

The stranger cut him off, saying, "Now, look real close in the center of your palm. If you try, you will see four faint lines that touch all the rest and form a strange looking square. It's a trapezoid."

"I know what it is, sheesh," Omen sarcastically said.

"Good . . . 'Seer's' are the only ones that have that mark. 'Master Seer's' don't have any lines."

"Master Seers? What is that?"

"Never mind, you'll learn that later."

He let go of Omen's hand, and then showed him his. His had the same mark. Omen opened his mouth and was about to speak, but the stranger spoke faster. He knew what question was coming.

"I don't know what it means, or why we have it, but one Master Seer has said that it is the key to their dimension. That's all I know."

Omen noticed a girl wearing a sexy blue outfit, complete with mini skirt and fishnet stocking. She was checking him out.

"So tell me why they created this reality," he asked, waving his hands around, indicating the surroundings. "What do they want with us?"

"It is believed that this reality, our perception of the world around us, is a mirror of where we came from. Maybe, it's what is inherent in us, our primordial memories. A 'Master Seer' once told me that this reality was chosen because it was the most suitable one for our minds to function healthy in. For our bodies to grow, and our essence or energy to strengthen. This makes sense, because they are not after our physical body. No, they feed off of our essence. When our bodies die our essence is released. And it's then that they devour it, preventing it from its unknown journey. We are energy. That's what that one was trying to do to that girl, when I found you."

Omen remembered what had happen before. He remembered the train tracks, the car, the girl, and the strange spiritual being. He remembered 'seeing' for the first time.

"We have an advantage, we can affect them in both dimensions, theirs and our physical one. They, however, cannot take action against us in their natural form. In order for them to attack us they have to 'Skin', or mind control someone else to attack us, but only after they have 'Skinned' someone."

Omen gave the stranger a disgusted look. "You mean they have to remove someone's flesh?"

"No, remember the train operator? That's what happened to him, that's why he attacked us after we stopped the angel, he was 'Skinned'. In other words, the angel entered into his body, possessed him . . . took his skin. They don't like to do that unless they want to get us. It's hard on them, and it wastes the essence of the body they control. The essence gets spread out, making it impossible for any lurkers to consume. I can only hope that it reunites and completes its transcendence. We, us Seers, manipulate and replenish our essence. A normal human can't do that, so their body dies. The angel uses the host's essence to perform . . . manifest . . . and change reality in the same way that we do. I'll never forget the time, in Florida, when I was taking on this 'Skin'. The bastard had taken the body of a female jogger. It was a bitch of a fight . . . they are strong. But the girl suffered, she suffered real bad. By the time that it was over, her corpse looked like a flame-roasted raisin." He closed his eyes and reflected.

Omen sat silently and eyed him. As insane as it all sounded, he knew that the guy was speaking the truth. Still, he had many questions.

"What about faith, God, demons, and religion for that matter?"

The stranger opened his eyes and said, "Faith . . . faith is what hides the truth. It's the substitute for not seeing. When they don't want you to know what's real, when they don't have or want you to have the answers, they tell you just to have faith. I've seen way too much to have faith. Oh, God, why have you forsaken us? I haven't seen any God, kid. Demons are just angels. They've got worse attitudes and a different way of doing things. Demons seem to like our playground better, they like to 'Skin' . . . just for the hell of it. For some reason they like humans who have *strong hate* going on inside them. Maybe, they are rebelling against their own kind. Now, what was the last thing you mentioned? Aww, yes, religion. Maybe, it's something humans have always needed. I know it's helped to hide their true motives and purpose."

As Omen listened to him, he started to turn an idea over in his head. It was a horrifying thought.

"So is that why people who have had a 'near-death experience' sometimes claim to have seen angels? And people have been led to believe that these angels are there to guide them into the next realm . . . but oh my fucking Jesus, they're not really there to help them! They're only there to destroy them!" It was a scary concept, he thought. Even more terrifying because he had seen it.

"Now, you're starting to see the big picture."

The blond haired stranger leaned forward against the table. It almost looked like he was trying to reach under the table and rub Omen's knee. Omen looked at him strangely for a moment.

"Here take this," the stranger said, and nodded downward at the table, suggesting that there was something underneath that he wanted to give to him. Omen slowly felt for something, until he finally touched an object that was hard and metal.

"It's an Auto Mag, loaded and ready. I've got to make a phone call," he said, and basically pushed it into Omen's hand.

The stranger, without further word, got up and elbowed his way through the crowded nightclub. Omen immediately stuffed the gun into his pants, pulling his 'NWO' tee-shirt over it. He prayed that it wouldn't discharge a round by accident. He especially liked being male. He glanced around the room like a kid who was trying to hide a porno-magazine from his mother, whom had just walked unexpectedly into his bedroom. He didn't know the first thing about firearms.

"Hi," someone said from behind him.

He quickly turned his head in the direction of the voice. It was a beautiful girl. He recognized her as the girl that was staring him down before. Her face was painted with vibrant colors and her light brown hair was teased out in a kind of retro-eighties fashion. His eyes directed themselves from her breasts to her smile and then back to her breasts. She saw it and grinned. She's hot, he thought to himself. He ran his hand over top of his head, wiping the sweat off of his forehead and in the process fixing his hair.

"I was watching you. You're a cutie," she said, innocently moving just enough to make her breast's jiggle.

Omen, acting cool, rubbed his chin and said, "What's your name, babe?"

"Mitzy." She pinched a strand of her hair and pulled it between her lips.

"I'm Omen," he told her, and reached out to take her hand. She touched his softly.

"Wow, you have strong hands," she said, as she looked down at his. Just as she started to turn his hand over, another hand grabbed hers and jerked it away.

"I'm sorry honey, but he's taken," the stranger said, giving her an evil grin.

"I see," she said, and then rolled her eyes. She looked at Omen and then walked away. Omen looked disappointed.

The stranger sat down and said, "Yeah, she's kick'n, but she's most likely a 'Siren'."

"A what?"

"A 'Siren', a whistle. It's what the angels sometimes use as radar . . . a tracking device. And that means that they're looking for us, and they're in the vicinity."

"Oh, I thought you were trying to say that she was a looker," he said with laughter. Omen stopped laughing a few seconds later because what the stranger had said finally sank in.

"Shit! She was a 'Skin'?"

"No, just a victim of a mind-link. There's a good chance that someone in every building, within a few city blocks, is looking for us right now at this very moment."

"What the fuck are we going to do?" Omen asked, and at the same time went for the gun.

"We'll try to lose them. I have a diversion working for us. With some luck we'll evade them, because we have something to do." He stood up and said, "Let's go."

Omen rose up and followed.

They hurried to one of the side door exits, and as Omen was leaving he caught a glimpse of the girl who had told him that her name was Mitzy. She was standing near one of the dancing cages, nursing a drink. She was looking at him, and his libido was going off the wall.

In the alley, Omen noticed the wet concrete and realized that it had been raining. A little ways down, the stranger climbed onto a black and silver colored sports motorcycle and started it up. Omen froze. He stared down at the ground engrossed in mysterious thoughts.

Did it really rain? Or is someone wanting me to think that it did? I'm confused. This is bullshit! What's really real?

He powerfully concentrated on the ground before him, until his mind was absorbed into that one single thought. *What's real?* An astonishing change occurred. The ground began to shimmer like when looking across a scorching hot desert road, the haze of the pounding heat. The ripple stretched the concrete into absurd proportions, and then in a blinding flash of bluish-white light snapped back. But the ground wasn't there! With his eyes wide open—almost to the point of popping out—he gazed into an immense abyss. It was a vast structure of endless gigantic iron beams, layers of massive metal reaching into eternal space. Molten green liquids coated them, sliding and dripping down onto the next.

Frightened, Omen stepped backward and bumped into the wall.

"Come on, hurry!" the stranger called to him.

As if having been slapped in the face, Omen spun his head toward the stranger. He ran over and jumped onto the bike. They road through the night cloaked streets.

The fence bordering the closed public park was bent from where the two had entered. The trespassers were enjoying a little horseplay in the pool water. Being just teenagers, meant that they had broken the law twice tonight. The other was curfew. One of the boys had his mind set on committing another one, a crime much more serious.

They had taken off their shirts and pants, and had dove into the chilly water.

"So Carl, I heard something," Simon said placing his hands on his friend's shoulders.

Water swished around, slapping them both in the face. Carl had to lift his chin and spit water in order to respond.

"Huh, what did you hear?" Carl questioned, still laughing a little.

"I heard you tried to fuck my girlfriend!"

Carl felt Simon's fingers apply more pressure, and he could see a look of venom in his buddy's eyes. "Whaaa . . . what? That's crazy, I'd never . . ."

They looked at each other, in silence, for almost a minute. Water sloshed around, caused by the movement of their kicking feet, and made a kerplunk sound as it hit the surrounding concrete edge. The light of the moon created an evil enhancement in lines forming on Simon's face.

"I don't believe you . . . Carl!" Simon suddenly screamed. He became an insane 'machine of rage' as he pushed Carl below the surface of the water. Simon's hands locked around Carl's throat. Carl, caught off guard, had taken a large gulp of water into his mouth and was choking. He flailed his fists out at Simon, hitting him in the arms and chest. Simon was holding him down, and he wasn't about to stop. He had never felt so strong in all his life. After minutes of struggling, Carl went unconscious, his lungs motionless—full of water. Simon continued to hold him under, squeezing his neck, until Carl's body began to float toward the top. Then he let go.

The stranger parked the motorcycle next to a children's slide, and then walked over to Omen.

"That's a fast bike," Omen said.

"Yeah, a 640 Duke II, nothing can beat that speed," the stranger said, looking around the dark park-grounds.

"Why are we here . . . in the park?" Omen asked. The surrounding darkness, interrupted by light lamps, in the after-hours.

"Because this is where 'EchoSage', a 'Master Seer', said it would happen," the stranger said in a manner that suggested Omen should have somehow already known that.

"Huh? Where what would happen?"

"Someone's going to die."

"How would the 'Master Seer' know that?"

They continued to walk side by side. Omen noticed the stranger looking in every direction, but mostly skyward. He had a daunting feeling come over him. Something was out there, something bad was going to happen, he kept thinking. Why am I out here in the park, at night, with a guy who hunts angels, or what ever the hell he thinks they are? I don't want to be here, I've got my music, my band. I've got a normal . . . well semi-normal life to lead. His mind was in a chaotic stir.

"A 'Master Seer' can see not only through the dimensional barrier as we do, but can also see through space and time. Some people call it remote-viewing. Each 'Master Seer' is different. Some have greater capability than others. Some have better clarity in their sight. EchoSage is a good friend."

"So they know when a person is going to die?"

"They can locate a general area where an essence is trickling. The furthest in time that I've known a 'Master Seer' to see, has been two days in advance. Who knows what those life-sucking creatures see. They can't see the physical like we do, at least not until they 'Skin'. You'll see, once we use our essence to attack them that's when they'll notice us."

"I don't think I want to see . . ."

But before he could elaborate on what he felt, the stranger grabbed the back of his collar and pointed ahead of them. About fifty yards away, just beyond a brick recreation building, he saw what looked something like a fireworks' show. It was the same eruption of red light that he had seen burst out of the girl's body, the girl that had given him a ride, before flipping the car close to the railroad, and before meeting the stranger. The best way to describe the spectacle, that he could think of, was to liken it to a giant 'sparkler'—those light-sticks kids love to twirl on the 'Fourth of July'—but fifty times bigger and more intense.

"Come on, we have to hurry. The essence, from what I've witnessed, takes about five to ten minutes in our dimension's time to awaken and make the full transition to the other-side." the stranger said, and started to sprint, tugging Omen along with him.

Omen ran along side of him up the grass hill. The uncomfortable feeling of the gun tucked inside his pants, hitting his groin and upper thighs as he ran, prompted him to remove it. Suddenly, a strong malevolent force rushed over him, like standing on the ocean shore and getting smacked by a killer-wave. Then he saw them! White-colored winged apparitions, flying specters . . . angelic hallucinations. Moving at an incredible speed toward the red gushing light. His senses became overwhelmed with evil . . . the grip of terror. He fell, sliding feet first, dropping the Auto-Mag. The stranger stopped and helped him up.

"They can't see us, get up!" the stranger barked, hefting Omen off the ground.

He was shaking as he retrieved the weapon and resumed the race. They stood a few feet away from the building—its walls decorated with graffiti—on top of the hill, overlooking a fenced in swimming pool. It was a mind-blowing sight. In the water, a body was floating face down, and from it an electrical explosion of brilliant dazzling red illumination issued forth . . . a volcanic eruption of the deceased's life-force. Climbing out, on the far side of the pool, was a young man wearing only his underwear. And above the water, circling like vultures, were five angels . . . waiting predators. The image was a shocking phantasmagoria. They were beings, human-like with large body length bird wings, dressed in elegant flowing vestments, each one of them having an attractive face. They reminded Omen of dolls—representations of human beings—affirming the statement that the stranger had made about them being something else . . . insidious man-eating monsters, who's true appearance was unknown.

Omen looked over at the stranger and asked, "What can we do to stop them?"

"You get the kid and I'll worry about them," he said.

Omen wondered what the stranger actually wanted him to do with the kid, who at the moment was getting dressed. He could tell that the kid didn't notice the essence and the lurkers above. The stranger was gone . . . almost to the fence, by the time he started to move. Omen hotfooted it down the hill, holding the gun in his right hand. He felt like an action hero . . . a bogus one. He was no hero, he thought. The kid had seen the stranger, and started running before Omen could get to him. He'd have to chase him down, or maybe . . . he wouldn't.

"Stop fucker, or I'll blow your head off!" Omen screamed as he pursued the runner.

Simon stopped dead in his tracks, turning his head around to see who was following him.

"Okay, okay, don't shoot man," Simon said, and held his arms up in surrender.

Omen stopped running and began to cautiously walk toward him, aiming the gun.

"I'm warning you, don't run or I'll waste you," Omen said.

"What do you want? I didn't do anything."

The stranger dexterously climbed the fence. He looked upon them with intense hatred. Standing near the edge of the swimming pool, he clasped his hands together. To an onlooker it would have appeared as though he was performing some kind of a martial artist's mantra. And in reality, he was in fact summoning power through his own essence. He squinted his eyes shut, cringing as if in pain . . . focusing . . . willing. Then, he thrust up his hands, palms forward, fingers open. From them, a light identical to the one coming out of the body in the water, streamed forth. It was an attack that he was well experienced at. It was the only way to harm them, the only way to reach into their dimension. He directed the outpour of essence at the angels. The assault strike hit them by surprise, every one of them consecutively consumed by the red flow, like electrical current conductors. The stranger's essence stabilized their movement, paralyzing them as the energy seemed to fuse itself into them. He yelled out as he struggled to maintain the surge. Five of them were a lot to take on. He began to doubt if he'd be able to stop them.

Omen heard the stranger's cry. He had the kid on his knees, covering him with the gun. He didn't know what to do. Should he let the kid run and go see what was happening? Or should he stay put and guard him? The sane thing to do would be to run like hell with the kid, he thought to himself.

"I didn't kill Carl . . . you've got to believe me," Simon pleaded.

"Really?" Omen said.

"Yeah, I think he hit his head when he jumped into the pool. I was going to go tell you."

"Tell me?" Omen asked surprised.

"Yeah you're a cop, ain't ya?"

Omen started to laugh, but just before letting it out, something slammed into the kid. It hit him with unbelievable force, knocking him back a good twenty feet! To Omen, it looked like the kid had been struck by an anti-tank missile, the blinding burst of light made him shield his eyes with his forearm and stumble backward. After a second or two, he lowered his arm. The kid was standing and facing him. His eyes were emitting rays of diabolical black energies. Omen's mind and body froze. Immobilized by fear, he watched and listened as the kid came toward him.

"You want to see me human! I'll fucking rip your eyes out and devour your motherfucking soul!" the kid growled at him.

An unbelievable thing happened next. The kid's arms transformed into long serrated deadly-looking metal blades. Omen saw the red energy—that he had come to identify as essence—being released, he remained in a state of shock. It charged him, swiftly running his left shoulder through with one of the freakish weapons. Omen immediately screamed in agony, feeling a crippling burning pain shoot up the left side of his neck. The attacker raised the other blade above his head, poised to strike Omen in the face. Then Omen remembered the gun. He stuck it into the kid's face and pulled the trigger. He spent the whole magazine, rapid fire. The eight rounds quickly made Swiss cheese out of his head, and took him down hard. Around the kid's head a cloud of essence formed a whirlpool, churning and rising into the air. Omen placed his right hand over his wounded shoulder, dropping the gun in the process. He felt his own warm sticky blood seeping out of the hole where the blade had torn his flesh. It hurt like hell, he thought. Or maybe it doesn't, he thought and kept thinking about it. He closed his eyes and centered his mind on the pain. He began to visualize the damaged muscle tissues, veins, blood vessels, and skin. He imagined that they were healing, joining together into their original state. When he finally opened his eyes, he removed his hand and to his amazement the injury has disappeared. He stared at the blood on his hand and shoulder. He had done it. Then he thought about what else he had done, he had killed someone. How would he be able to explain it to the police, he thought panicking. He had to find the stranger. He started to walk, but had to struggle not to fall down. He suddenly realized how fatigued and out of energy he was . . . it felt strange. So worn out in fact, that he dropped down to one knee.

With his back turned toward the young man's body, he couldn't see it when it rose up. The kid, whose face had become a bloodied mangle of ripped flesh, mutated into a demonic-looking reptilian creature twice his normal size. It opened a large threatening mouth, full of razor sharp teeth like that of a crocodiles, and lurched forward reading to attack its unaware victim.

"Omen, get down!" the stranger hollered. Omen saw him coming forward out of the darkness, wielding an assault rifle. He dove forward, and buried his face into the grass. Face down, with the scent of earth-soil invading his nostrils, he heard the spray of ammunition flying over him. It was fierce, he covered his ears with his hands. The gunfire lasted forever, or so it seemed.

Omen felt a nudge and uncovered his ears.

"You can get up now," the stranger said.

Lifting his head up, he saw that the stranger was sitting in the grass beside him. He looked beat.

"You okay?" the stranger asked.

"Yeah. Are you?" Omen asked.

"I've been through worse and survived."

Omen sat up and glanced over at the body of the young man, lying about thirty feet away.

"How will we explain it?" Omen asked with his eyes fixed on the body.

"We won't have to," the stranger said, in that cool sounding voice, Omen had come to be familiar with. "Just give me some time to rest . . . five of them was more than I had expected."

"Did we win?"

"Yeah."

"You know you never did tell me your name," Omen said with a smile.

The stranger gave him a hard look and then said, "You never asked. You can call me Elijah Lydon, but all my friends call me the *Angel Killer.*"

"Okay, then get me some food and a nice soft bed . . . *Angel Killer.*"

Dining at Sea by Steven E. Wedel

Raymond wasn't sorry most of the other men had drowned. He was only sorry that Manuel hadn't gone to the bottom of the Pacific with them. The Mexican, or Puerto Rican, or whatever he was, sat across from Raymond in the yellow inflatable raft, his hairy brown arms thrown out, resting on the sides of the raft, his legs spread before him. Manuel was probably in his late forties and was always grinning—a mean grin that split his raggedly-bearded face and showed off his perfect, gleaming teeth.

"Maybe you should paddle with your hands, no?" Manuel said.

Raymond started to answer, then stopped himself. It was useless to fight with the other man. He had already struggled against his captors and bore the bruises to prove it. Manuel outweighed Raymond by at least a hundred pounds and, if worse came to worse, Manuel still had his long knife strapped to his waist. Raymond was sure Manuel didn't have any qualms about using the knife.

"You don't want to paddle, I think." Manuel nodded.

"There's nothing to paddle with. We couldn't get anywhere with just our hands.

"Somebody sent a distress call, didn't they? Somebody will find us."

Manuel laughed. "Nobody on the Lucifer sent a distress call. We are smugglers. Most of us are wanted men. I am worth one hundred thousand dollars to your FBI." Manuel nodded proudly.

"Smugglers." Raymond rubbed the back of his head where one of his captors had knocked him out before dragging him onto the doomed yacht. "Why did you bring me? What do you do, sell slaves, too?"

"Sometimes the captain, he likes to bring hostages," Manuel said, nodding and grinning again. "Sometimes it is good to have a hostage. I think that is why you are here."

"It was you that hit me outside the bar, wasn't it."

Manuel only grinned. They drifted in silence.

Slowly, the sun sank into the sea, leaving only a pale blush to the sky. Stars began to twinkle overhead, growing brighter as the blush faded, making the sky a smooth velvet cloth over the rippling silk of the sea, both alive with glittering diamonds.

"Where were we going?" Raymond asked.

"North."

"North? Why north?"

"I am not the captain. I do not know."

More silence. More darkness. Raymond heard his stomach growl. There was no food in the raft—no water, either. Raymond wanted to sleep, but was afraid to do so with Manuel awake. His eyelids sagged. He forced them open. They closed again. He jerked awake, and noticed something bobbing in the waves about thirty yards to the northwest of the raft.

"What's that?" Raymond plunged his hands into the water and started paddling in the direction of the object. To his surprise, Manuel leaned over the side of the raft and added his efforts. Raymond watched the Hispanic's muscles bulge and ripple as he paddled. He wondered if he could get the knife away from Manuel if it came to that.

"It's a box," Raymond gasped as they drew closer. The box was about eight feet long and three feet wide. It had two steel eyes on each end; a short piece of thick rope was still tied to one of the eyes.

"I remember this," Manuel said. "Yes, this was on the Lucifer. I helped to load it from the dock and put it in the hold."

"What's in it?" Raymond asked. "Is that what you were smuggling?"

"No, no, it couldn't be." Manuel shook his shaggy head. "It is too light, see? I think it is empty. See how it rides high on the water. It must be empty. You are stupid to not see that."

"Why would you carry an empty box?"

"I do not know why," Manuel snapped. "I told you already, I am not the captain." He started to push the box away, but Raymond grabbed the rope and tied it to one of the raft's oar locks. "Why do you do that? I don't want to drag this with us."

"I do."

Manuel's hand raised to his knife but stopped. Raymond acted as if he hadn't noticed, but he tried to prepare himself for the fight. "You are a foolish little man," the Hispanic hissed. "I look forward to eating you and drinking your blood to keep myself alive."

"I would be a very unhealthy meal for you." Raymond hoped he sounded tough. Manuel laughed at him.

They drifted quietly for a while. Raymond kept looking at the box, trying to figure out what was wrong with it. Finally he realized what he'd been looking for.

"There's no nails or screws in the top of this box," he said. He reached out and pushed at the top panel, but it didn't move. "How do you think it's fastened?"

"I don't care," Manuel said. "I am getting hungry. Maybe I will cut a piece at a time to keep you alive until I have to kill you. I like my meat to be fresh. I could cut off a leg below the knee tonight, the other tomorrow, then the arms—"

Raymond couldn't bear it any longer. "Shut up, you damn spick," he shouted. "Shut your fucking mouth. You want to kill me? Go ahead and do it now. Come on. I'd rather die now than have to sit here and smell you and listen to you until we're rescued."

Again, Manuel laughed. He threw back his head so that he was nearly lying in the bottom of the raft and cackled like a woman. Then he stopped abruptly and showed Raymond his evil grin. "I am not so hungry yet," he said. "I will kill you when I am ready. Perhaps when you are sleeping, no?"

Raymond jumped on him. Manuel was ready for him, however, and knocked Raymond aside, then rose to his knees and drew his knife. Raymond threw himself forward, into the Hispanic's body. He felt the knife tear his shirt and heard a sudden hiss as the blade plunged into the bottom of the rubber raft.

"Now look what you've done, you stupid son of a bitch," Raymond yelled.

Manuel didn't answer. He pulled his knife out and jabbed it at Raymond's stomach. Raymond dodged the blade again, but Manuel's fist found the side of his head. Raymond fell onto his side. The air escaping from the raft gushed into his face. The knife was coming again. Raymond grabbed Manuel's wrist. He couldn't stop the descent, but he guided it away from his body. The blade slashed across two more chambers of the raft. More air rushed out and suddenly the raft was filling with salty water. Manuel fell sideways as the raft sagged. Raymond used all his strength to shove his opponent off him and into the water.

Manuel yelled something in Spanish as he fell. The knife flew out of his hand and stuck into another of the raft's air chambers. Manuel flailed in the water; Raymond realized the Hispanic couldn't swim, but didn't try to help him.

Raymond grabbed the knife and stuck it into his own belt as the raft became nothing but a dancing yellow stain beneath the waves, the one undamaged air chamber like a bubble on the surface of the ocean. He grabbed hold of the floating box and held on, listening to Manuel's bubbling screams.

The lid of the box flew open and a man sat up in it. Raymond's fingers slipped away and he nearly sank into the ocean at the sudden appearance of the new figure. The man reached out and grabbed Manuel from the water, dragging him into the box as if he were a huge, limp rat.

"Dear God in Heaven," Raymond whispered as the stranger tilted Manuel's head back and lowered his own long teeth to the hairy brown throat. The man rolled his eyes to stare at Raymond as he drank the blood of Manuel. Raymond could see the color draining from Manuel's body as the blood was taken. Then it was over. The stranger, the vampire, pushed the body out of the box and into the sea. With a long-fingered, thin hand, he beckoned to Raymond. Raymond shook his head and turned to swim away.

"Where will you go, my friend?" The vampire's voice was filled with humor, almost mocking, but too silky to be cruel. "Come back. I have fed for the night and you are safe. Come back. Sit in my box with me."

Raymond stopped swimming and turned back to face the vampire. His box—his coffin—still rode high on the waves, the lid standing straight up so that the vampire, a pale man in a dark, modern suit with a silk tie, leaned his shoulder against it.

"You won't kill me?" Raymond asked.

"Not tonight." The vampire smiled and Raymond saw that his teeth were still stained with Manuel's blood. The vampire beckoned with his hand again. Reluctantly, Raymond swam back to the coffin, where the vampire hauled him into the box just as he had lifted Manuel. Raymond sensed the creature's incredible strength as he was lifted clear of the water.

Manuel's body was bobbing away from them on the dark ocean. Raymond didn't feel pity for the man. He was too concerned with his own safety. He sat up in the coffin, crossed his legs before him, and faced the vampire.

"I heard most of your conversation with the other," the vampire said, waving a hand toward Manuel's corpse. "I think Captain Davis took you onto his ship to feed me on the long journey north. He chose well." The vampire smiled.

"I'm not comforted by that," Raymond said.

"No, I don't guess you would be." The vampire smiled again. "You asked why we were going north. I will tell you. In the far north, the nights last for months during this time of the year. It is always dark. I wanted to see if I would feel the need to retreat to my coffin if the sun did not rise."

"There aren't many people that far north," Raymond said. "I mean—"

"What would I feed on?" The vampire laughed—a low, rippling sound. "There are not many people, no, and there would have been less if I had reached my destination."

"What are we going to do now?" Raymond asked. "What are you going to do with me?"

"This box we are in is sealed against the water," the vampire said. "We will wait in it. Eventually a ship will find us, or we will wash up on shore."

"But—" Raymond wasn't sure what to say. "You're a vampire. I mean, when they open the lid, if it's daylight—"

"A risk, true." The vampire nodded. "But, as you noticed, there are no nails or screws visible on the outside of the box. It latches from the inside. Most people would spend a great deal of time studying the box before risking its destruction with a forced entry. By then, hopefully, the sun will be gone from the sky."

"You said we. Do you mean for me to—to lie in there with you?"

"Yes, I do." The vampire did not smile now. He fixed Raymond with his deep black eyes and held him. "We could be on the sea for a long time. If you were not in here with me, but say, riding on top of the coffin when we are found, you could alert our rescuers to the contents of this box and destroy me. And, of course, I will be hungry again every night."

"Hungry?"

"Your friend spoke of eating you. His methods were crude. I can feed on you night after night without killing or maiming you. I will take only what I need. When we are rescued, I can make you a vampire . . . or I can kill you, as you wish."

Raymond couldn't answer. He stared at the vampire. Suddenly he sprang to his feet and jumped out of the coffin, prepared to swim away and face drowning rather than the choices of the undead.

But the vampire was faster than Raymond. He caught Raymond by the ankle and dragged him back into the coffin. He forced Raymond to the bottom of the box and lay over him with his own body, like a man mounting a woman. Raymond's struggles were useless against the powerful creature.

"Perhaps you will change your mind before we are rescued, my friend," the vampire said as he pulled the lid of the coffin closed.

The stars were suddenly gone. Raymond heard several muffled clicks and knew the vampire was sealing the box from the inside. The vampire was still on top of him, almost weightless, but Raymond could not move him.

"Be still." The vampire covered Raymond's mouth with a cool, dry hand. "Sleep."

After a time, Raymond did. When he awoke, the vampire was slumped over him like a lifeless corpse. Raymond fidgeted, but the vampire did not move or speak. Raymond raised his hands until he was sure they were over his face and pushed the button that made the dial of his watch light up. He guessed he had slept for close to ten hours. It was daylight outside the box, and the vampire was in his forced sleep.

With the life out of him, the vampire was much heavier than he had been. Raymond struggled to get out from under the body, finally settling with his back against the side of the box, the vampire sleeping beside him.

Raymond slid his hands along the top of the box, hoping to find the latches so he could open the lid, letting in the fatal sunlight. He found one, felt the cold metal, but he could not figure out how to work the mechanism. In the total darkness, he couldn't even study the lock to try to understand it. From touch, he determined it was unlike any latch he knew.

He tried pounding on the lid, hoping to force it up, but that was useless.

Something was pressing against Raymond's thigh. He reached down and found the handle of Manuel's long knife.

It wasn't a wooden stake like they used to kill the undead in movies, but Raymond felt pretty sure the vampire couldn't survive without his head. He drew the knife and felt for the vampire's throat with his other hand while he wriggled his body toward the foot of the coffin to give his arms more striking room. Raymond took a deep breath, then stabbed the knife into the vampire's throat and prepared to saw with the blade.

The vampire convulsed violently. He arms and legs flailed, bruising Raymond as they battered him. The vampire's upper torso and head jerked up and down, banging the coffin as his hands and feet pounded the wooden confines.

Raymond struggled to avoid being hammered, but couldn't get out of reach of the arms and legs. He tried to get into a fetal position to protect his head.

Then he heard the wood crack. The vampire had split the wood of the coffin's bottom with his head. Water rushed into the box. The vampire continued convulsing.

"Stop it! Stop it! Open the fucking box!" Raymond yelled. He reached up and ran his hands along the lid, feeling for the strange latches. The vampire's knee came up suddenly and connected with his hand; Raymond heard the snap as several of his fingers were smashed and broken between the vampire's knee and the coffin lid. He howled with the pain and sea water filled his mouth.

The head of the coffin was tilted down and filling fast. Raymond put out his hands to brace himself against that end of the coffin, the vampire beneath him now, still jerking. The water rose above his arms. Raymond took a deep breath as the water rushed over his head. He felt the coffin start racing toward the bottom of the ocean as the water rose to his feet.

"At least no one's going to eat me," Raymond thought. He had one last idea.

Raymond pushed at the bottom of the coffin where the vampire's head had cracked the wood. The bottom of the box was split from head to foot. Raymond braced his back against the lid and pushed with both hands and his knees at one half of the split bottom. The wood gave way suddenly and Raymond slipped out of the opening, tangling with the vampire as he did.

He couldn't hold his breath any longer. The air gushed out of his burning lungs. He breathed in, tasting salt water mingled with the blood flowing from the vampire's throat.

Raymond shoved the body away and started swimming toward the surface, a ribbon of the vampire's blood wound around him as he struggled against the water. The vampire rose toward the surface, too, toward the brightening ceiling of light. Raymond thought he could see the body beginning to smoulder even in the water.

He never saw the shark that was attracted by the scent of the vampire's blood and the vibrations of his own swimming. He tried to scream as the rows of deadly teeth sank into his right thigh and the shark dragged him deeper into the cold Pacific.

Rampart by Amy Grech

An old man named Charles Rampart with snow-white hair wearing glasses as thick as slices of bread sat hunched in a winged-backed chair engrossed in a good book. A fire flickered lazily in the fireplace to his right; its warmth kept him company.

Every so often he would set the book in his lap and glance nervously around the room, checking to see that the vase in the far corner was still even with the edge oriental rug in the center of his study. The dim light made it nearly impossible to tell, but when Charles squinted, he swore the vase didn't line up anymore, that it had moved closer to the center of the room when the walls started closing in.

His beloved wife, Susan, humored him, convinced that senility caused his paranoia. It never occurred to her that there might actually be something to fear . . .

Susan tiptoed into Charles's study, being careful not to startle him, and extinguished the fire. Then she set the book on the end table next to his chair and coaxed him upstairs to bed. All the while, he stared at the floor, unable to bear the dreadful sight of the walls advancing ever so slowly.

His wife frowned. "What's wrong now?" She took his hand and held it tight.

He worked up the nerve to look around. "I do believe my castle is trying to destroy me. The walls are closing in as we speak." His voice was as shaky as his movements.

Susan raised her eyebrows. "Don't be ridiculous."

Charles pointed a trembling finger at the vase. "Look, that vase isn't even with the rug anymore. It was this afternoon. How do you explain that?"

"You must be seeing things." Susan bit her lip, troubled by her husband's startling observation.

The next morning, Charles woke early and felt rested enough to venture downstairs alone to the kitchen. Not wanting to wake Geoff, the butler, he prepared a feast of scrambled eggs, bacon, French toast, orange juice, and coffee for Susan and himself. Charles placed everything on an enormous tray and set it down on the dining room table, trying hard not to look at the walls along the way.

Much to his dismay, they had moved again. He was certain of it; early in the morning, the picture of Susan at the far end of the room was even with the china cabinet, but now it was much closer to the dining room table. When the wall that housed the picture moved, the cabinet inched forward, so that it was no longer even with the table.

Frantic, he ran upstairs to get his wife, who had just finished dressing and met him in the hallway.

"What is it now?" Susan took him by the hand and led him downstairs, afraid he might trip and tumble down headfirst in such an agitated state.

"The walls moved again!" Like a frightened child, Charles cringed, wide-eyed.

She sighed, tired of these grueling episodes. "Show me where."

"In the dining room." He led her to the scene of the incident.

Susan went over to the china cabinet and was surprised to see that it had indeed moved. She shook her head. "Geoff must have moved things around to vacuum."

"Let's ask him and put my mind at ease." Charles yanked the chord that rang a bell in the servants' quarters and waited.

Moments later, the distinguished butler appeared, dressed in a tuxedo. "You rang?"

"Yes, Geoff. Did you clean the dining room yesterday?" Charles cocked his head, anxious for a logical explanation.

With a furrowed brow he nodded. "Of course. Did I do an unsatisfactory job?"

Susan smiled and spoke before her husband could get a word in. "Not at all, but I do have one question: Did you forget to put the china cabinet back where it belonged?"

"No, for some strange reason there didn't seem to be enough room to move it back, or else I would have." Geoff scratched his head, quite puzzled.

Charles folded his arms. "See, I told you the walls moved! I'm a doomed man!"

"Calm down." His wife went over to the offending wall and leaned against it, but it didn't budge. "See, this wall is as solid as the rocks it was built with."

"Then why did the china cabinet move?" Charles's eyes darted around the room, searching for answers but finding none.

Susan was at a loss for words.

"I think I can explain." Geoff grinned. "Why don't you sit down and have your breakfast while I tell you a story that might help put things into perspective."

Charles and Susan did as they were told.

The butler sat at the head of the table and cleared his throat before he told his tale: "When I started working here thirty years ago, your grandfather was the proud owner of this castle. He had it built during the Depression and wanted everything to be authentic, so he had these stones imported from England. Little did he know that most of them, especially the ones on the second floor, were actually headstones filched from local graveyards, stolen from their rightful owners, the dearly departed." Geoff shook his head. "Some people have no respect for the dead."

Charles polished off his eggs. "Can you prove what you say is true? Were you there when it happened?"

"Indeed I was. I didn't actually do any of the stealing, but I had the grim task of supervising the project. I certainly didn't enjoy it, but I had little choice in the matter; I had a wife and children to feed." Geoff went over to the other end of the room and pointed to one of the stones near the picture. "Come over here, I'll show you what I mean. May I suggest that the walls are being moved by the headstones' former owners, who are merely trying to reclaim what's rightfully theirs, without any regard for the living? It seems only logical, since the grave robbers didn't think the headstones would be missed. I think it's safe to say they were sadly mistaken."

Charles stood up and crossed the room, leaning on Susan for support. "Ghosts? That's ridiculous! Why would they wait so long to seek revenge?"

The butler shrugged. "Perhaps they ran out of patience."

They stared at the flat rock Geoff pointed to and were shocked by what they saw carved on the stone: barely legible were these words: HERE LIES RICHARD RAMPART 1876 - 1938.

"He was my grandfather! I'm done for!" Overwhelmed by the truth, Charles clutched his chest and collapsed.

Susan screamed.

Geoff dialed 911.

An ambulance arrived minutes later. The paramedics agreed to let Susan ride in the back with her husband. When they arrived at the hospital, the prognosis was encouraging. The doctor told Susan Charles had suffered a mild heart attack and would have to be kept overnight for observation. Sedated, he slept soundly. His wife stayed by his side until the doctor decided he was well enough to be discharged the following morning.

"Feeling better?" Geoff greeted them at the front door when the silver Rolls Royce pulled up.

Charles winked. "Quite."

Susan pulled Geoff aside. "Dr. Heartwell said he needs plenty of bed rest and no more surprises."

"Understood." The butler nodded.

She helped Charles up to the bedroom while Geoff prepared lunch.

Charles paused in the hallway, checking the stones for inscriptions. Finding one that was illegible but still visible, he flinched. "The walls have moved again!" With trembling fingers, he touched the stone, feeling its roughness and permanence of the letters etched upon it.

Susan tightened her grip on his arm. "No they haven't." Feeling cynical, she didn't bother to check, because she wanted to believe that Charles was imagining the whole incident. "You're still delirious. Come on, you need to rest."

She led him into the bedroom, took off his shoes, and helped him into bed.

He struggled to sit up. "I'm hungry. Where's my lunch?"

"I'll ring Geoff and have him bring it up." Susan gave the chord next to the bed a firm tug.

The butler appeared with a tray of cucumber sandwiches and two glasses of lemonade, his favorite meal.

"Lunch is served." He set it down on the bed, next to Charles.

"Thank you, Geoff. You may go now." Susan smiled and sat down on the edge of the bed.

He bowed and left the room.

Charles devoured half of the sandwiches in record time.

"You must be feeling better. I see your appetite is back. That's a good sign." Susan helped herself to a sandwich before Charles finished them all.

He shook his head. "I won't rest until I'm certain the walls have stopped moving."

"That might take less time than you think." She finished her lemonade and rang for the butler to come take the tray.

Charles blinked. "What do you mean?"

"Don't you remember what Geoff said about the dead seeking revenge?" Susan rolled her eyes and stood to go.

He shrugged. "Yes, but I don't believe it."

"But your grandfather's name was on that stone! Explain that." She paused at the door

"I can't. I think Geoff's story planted some crazy ideas in my head."

She laughed. "I don't think you have anything to worry about."

Susan went downstairs with Geoff, leaving Charles alone to think. He could feel the walls were advancing on him, he'd seen the proof, and he had no idea how to stop it.

Sighing, he took his glasses off and set them down on the nightstand. He shut his eyes and drifted off into a troubled sleep.

Charles dreamed he was reading in his study again when the walls suddenly started getting closer and closer together. It happened so fast he couldn't get out of his chair before being sandwiched between them with no hope of escape . . .

He awoke with a start and strained to see, until he realized he wasn't wearing his glasses. When Charles put them on, what he saw made him wish he were already dead: all four walls in the bedroom really had closed in silently while he slept. Frantic, he struggled to get up, but it was no use, the bed was wedged so tightly between them he couldn't move.

Charles strained to yank the chord until he heard Geoff and Susan rush upstairs to his aid. He clutched the bedcovers in trembling hands.

"Charles, honey, what's wrong?" When Susan jiggled the doorknob, the door didn't budge. "Come open the door."

He screamed, "I'M TRAPPED BETWEEN THE WALLS!! NOW DO YOU BELIEVE ME?!"

His wife gasped. "I'm so sorry I didn't listen, but the notion of the walls closing in seemed so unthinkable!"

The butler rushed over to the door with a crowbar and tried to pry it open. "Sir, try to calm down and tell us what happened."

Charles took a deep breath. "I must've dozed off after lunch, because when I woke up the bed was caught between the walls, and that's when I rang the bell."

Geoff and Susan threw their weight against the door, in a futile attempt to break it down; the wood didn't even splinter.

"Are the walls still moving, Charles?" Susan buried her face in her hands.

Charles's shriek was the only reply.

"I *knew* this would happen." The butler dropped the crowbar; it clattered and slipped between the cracks of a rapidly growing fissure in the cold, flagstone floor beneath him.

The Hotel of the Dead by Kevin James Miller

From the earliest moments of childhood, Harrison Baker had recurring dreams of a place he eventually named the Hotel of the Dead.

Harrison always dreamed in color. This was a trait shared by people with a vivid imagination, a compulsive subconsciousness. Perhaps out of a desire to control that quality in himself, he became a journalist. After that, he was professionally dedicated to finding out the truth, organizing the facts into reports and presenting them to the world.

He made his reputation by being one of the first journalists to file a report on "the Uniform Killer." This was a serial murderer who wore a series of rented costumes depicting himself as a surgeon, letter carrier, U.S. Army colonel, etc.—all as a ruse to get closer to his victims in order to strangle them. Harrison's story led to the arrest and conviction of the Uniform Killer, and the rogue escaped execution by reason of his manifest insanity—but got imprisonment nonetheless for his equally manifest evil.

Harrison Baker guided his career into print journalism, and passed over several opportunities to move into television, squeamish about the show business excesses he found inherited in the medium.

But before all that, before growing up, and life as a working adult, there was, in his dreaming life, the Hotel of the Dead.

It was a place of red walls and floors. The front desk was black, black as a sunless pit. There was a revolving door of glass and ancient wood, and the exterior of the hotel was gray mist. In the dreams he came in, approached the front counter and the front desk man, who had his back to Harrison Baker. The front desk man was dressed in a blue suit, and had short black hair.

He turned toward Harrison Baker and was some sort of outlandish ghoul. Much of the tissue of the face was gone, but not entirely, making the sight more unsettling than if it was just a simple Halloween prop. The remaining flecks of skin and muscle were nauseating to view. In addition, eyeballs, bloodshot and oily, rested in that bony face that was fleshy only in flecks and bits.

"Time to check in now, Mr. Baker?" asked the ghoul. Its voice was a rattling moan which hurt Harrison's teeth and gave him stomach aches.

Imagine being three years old and having such a dream—and it, and variations of it, following you into twelve, sixteen, twenty-seven, thirty-two, and forty.

By forty Harrison had a secured a position with the magazine. He had a degree of fame and success that would never measure up to what someone in film or sports could have, but which he found more than satisfactory.

The job gave him plenty of opportunity to travel. For example, he covered the civil war in Mahteeloh. In their part of Africa, the Mahteeloh-ahndi was a traditionalist tribe. They mixed easily with the other citizens, and it was a common sight to see the orange robe, spear-carrying Mahteeloh-ahndi walk the streets with the suit wearing, briefcase-carrying Mahteeloh tribe.

A member of the Mahteeloh tribe was the front desk man when Baker signed the guest register at a hotel called the Commons Inn.

When Baker looked up, he was in the Hotel of the Dead. The walls and floors were red, the front desk was black, and there was the revolving door of glass and ancient wood, and nothing but gray smoke outside. The ghoul from his nightmares was, at least, not present. What Harrison saw instead was the ordinary enough looking African gentleman who had been waiting on Harrison Baker a few seconds ago.

But the man behind the counter must have seen the distress in Harrison's face.

"Are you OK, Mr. Baker?"

Harrison Baker gasped, dropped the pen and took off his glasses. He closed and rubbed his eyes, and smoothed down his moustache, a nervous gesture he had picked up at nineteen and had never discarded.

When he opened his eyes, the Hotel of the Dead was gone. The lobby of this hotel, in the real country of Mahteeloh, in the real continent of Africa was back. So were its lime green walls, slowly revolving fan in the ceiling and combination phone booth, fax machine and computer with Internet connection in the corner.

That evening, Harrison started to walk to a bar about a mile away. His contacts had told him that if he wanted to understand what the situation was with the guerrillas there was a man he had to see who frequented the bar.

His last time in this part of Africa, Harrison had only picked up a wild, worthless rumor. It was something about two white men, tourists, who were in the city kidnaping children off the streets, and that was supposed to be the only reason these two traveled from country to country. The journalist thought this myth originated with the hostility of the guerrillas toward white Westerners.

Harrison hoped he wasn't going to run into the woman from the cable news service again. She was always trying to talk him into trying his hand at writing novels, something Harrison wasn't interested in.

He saw a member of the Mahteeloh-ahndi tribe walking on the other side of the street, walking along in the opposite direction. Harrison Baker was just smiling and nodding blankly at the Mahteeloh-ahndi, when the tribesman's eyes widened and he raised and hurled his spear at Harrison.

He jumped and the spear landed in a Mahteeloh. He wore blue jeans, a black T-shirt and a small skull around his neck on a gold chain and he held a large automatic pistol.

Harrison Baker knew the skull on the small gold chain was authentic and had belonged to a bat. It was common knowledge that such was the attire of the murderous bandit gangs that plagued the city he was in. In other words, the Mahteeloh-ahndi man had saved Harrison's life.

The rest of his stay was without such unsettling juxtapositions, but it was enough to plant shadowy seeds in his mind. The hallucination of the Hotel of the Dead, and almost being killed by the bandit he might have written off as coincidence, if it wasn't for another episode.

This other event also had its echo in a Hotel of the Dead nightmare. In one version of the nightmare, Harrison Baker had taken a room in the Hotel of the Dead and was getting room service. (Sometimes he had placed an order. Sometimes he got it without asking for it.)

The room service man was a ghoul as well, like the creature at the front desk, but not exactly. What came to Harrison's room, in the nightmare, had white and gray skin, and wore what looked like sewn together oil rags. It had all white eyes—in neither one no iris, no pupil, just white, like snow, like the paler parts of a diabolical television screen.

Then the room service ghoul rolled the service cart into Harrison's room. On the cart was a big covered dish. Harrison sat on the bed, in this version of the nightmare, anxious because he wasn't sure if he were wearing his glasses or not. He was afraid he had lost them, and he tried to feel them on his face and they seemed to be there, but not there at the same time.

When the cart was right in front of him, the room service ghoul lifted the cover of the dish.

It was a large bowl, and it was stuffed with people. There were clearly, by their appearance and proportions, adults, but not one of them was over three inches tall. Men, women, the young, the middle-aged, the elderly all struggled to get out of the bowl, but it was slick with what might have been blood, or red oil or a crimson and watery gelatine substance.

The magazine sent Harrison to Paris, to cover a business endeavor for an international TV network featuring philosophers.

He sat in a cafe. His host, a woman with the longest black hair he had ever seen on anybody, explained to him why, as a libertarian existentialist, she had Elvis tattooed on her arm.

While they waited for the waiter to come with their order, Harrison wondered why she wasn't married yet.

Lunch, at first, looked like the bowl with the little people struggling to get out of it.

With a scream, Harrison got to his feet. When he looked again, the bowl of tiny, struggling people was, instead, a salad.

Harrison wanted to accept his lady philosopher friend's offer and spend an evening at the theater to see the popular new farce from a Madrid playwright. However, he elected instead to stay in his hotel room and order up pornographic movies to watch.

Yes, it was that Paris performance—the one where most of the audience, including Harrison's new lady friend, the Elvis worshiping philosopher, were slaughtered by a neo-Nazi terrorist group.

Convinced that the Hotel of the Dead was now beginning to invade his life and with it, he felt sure, bring his immediate death, he persuaded his editors at the magazine to allow him several weeks vacation.

Harrison Baker decided not to go any place or do anything dangerous. He had taken plenty of reasonable risks before in his line of work, but he was convinced that forces from beyond this world had targeted him. He felt certain powers beyond time and space had marked him for termination.

Harrison was grateful for the awards and specialized celebrity of his profession, and the great nonsense of so-called glamour that occasionally floated around his job. However, journalism was a very practical business, which was why he had elected, years ago, to make his home in mundane suburbia.

One afternoon, Harrison was in his living room (a part of the house he had, for years, compulsively lingered in), reading an anthology of comic essays from the 1940's and the 1950's. He wiped some dirt off his glasses.

The doorbell rang.

He put the book on the floor, eased off the couch and tip toed over to the curtained window. He peaked out and saw, at the front door, a girl, about twelve years old. She was dressed in the blue skirt, white blouse and green beret of the Adventure Girls (a harmless organization that encouraged camping and good deeds for the young and female). She stood at Harrison's door. She had long blonde hair, and had several boxes of cookies tucked under her arm.

Or at least, that's the way everything looked. The girl, of course, could have had a small pistol on her person, and been ready to shoot Harrison dead as soon as he opened the door. Or Harrison could buy a box of cookies, and eat them, and they could turn out to be poisoned and he would then die.

He decided not to make things easier for the lurking presence of the Hotel of the Dead.

He smoothed down his moustache.

However, he did not want to become completely paranoid.

When the Adventure Girl rang again, he opened his door.

"Good afternoon." She smiled sweetly. "Want to buy some cookies, mister?"

"Yeah sure." He dug out his wallet and gave her a twenty. "Keep the change."

"Hey thanks!"

"Have a great day."

Harrison closed the door, and tossed the box of cookies up in the air and caught them. Although the occult had him in its sights, something like a box of cookies was probably innocent enough. He smiled, shrugged and looked out his front window, wanting to see the reassuring vision of a normal twelve-year-old girl walking away.

What he saw instead were the two ghouls from his nightmares pulling her into a long black car. The room service ghoul held her, with its hand over her mouth. The front desk ghoul drove the car, which sped away.

Furthermore, the creatures from the bowl, from the nightmares, were painted on the car.

Or images of them were, anyway. Of course the two ghouls were supposed to just be images also, just nightmare illusions.

Harrison ran to his phone, snatched up the receiver and froze.

What would he tell the 911 operator? Hi, two ghouls that have haunted my nightmares since I was a child have just snatched a little girl from in front of my house? Send a patrol car around, won't you? There's a good chap.

Not knowing what else to do, Harrison grabbed his car keys off the coffee table.

A little while later he was on the streets, and it was easy to find the car being driven by the ghouls, who still held their young captive.

Harrison chased the bad guys, although "enigmatically malevolent forces from beyond time and space" was more accurate.

His adversaries led him to a part of town where a lot of construction was going on, and traffic was light.

At one point, a police officer on a motorcycle started to chase Harrison, and the long black car. Harrison wondered if the cop had gotten a report about two monsters who had kidnaped a little girl off the street, possibly for the purpose of luring a 40-year-old journalist into some sort of trap.

No. None of this was making sense to Harrison, no matter how he tried to think of it.

Harrison and the cop on the motorcycle caught up to the ghoul car in the parking lot of what would one day be a retail store. Right at the moment, it was the metal frame of a building. The construction crew had gone home for the day. The sun was going down.

Then the journalist pulled up to the ghoul car as the black vehicle stopped.

Now what?

Harrison saw it was starting to get dark now.

In shadows, the occupants of the ghoul car sprung out of the doors of their machine . . .

. . . And fired guns in Harrison's direction? That was a little prosaic for nightmare ghouls, wasn't it?

Gunfire cracked from behind Harrison.

Harrison looked over his shoulder and the motorcycle cop held a smoking revolver. His motorcycle was parked several yards behind him. Gun still in his hand, wearing sunglasses and helmet, the cop strolled toward the ghoul car.

But that machine now looked pretty ordinary. Harrison walked over to the car as well, which no longer had the odd characters painted on it.

Two ordinary-looking men, both dead, both holding guns, laid by the long black car. They clearly had never been nightmare ghouls. They wore T-shirts, jeans and sneakers. One needed a shave, and one had bad teeth.

The little girl was in the back seat, crying.

"Are you OK?" asked the cop. "Did they hurt you?"

"I'm OK," the girl said. "Who are these bad men?"

"Never mind that now." He put his revolver in a hip holster. He took out two quarters and a business card, and gave the money and card to her. "You see that public phone, about a block from here? I want you to call this number and tell them what happened."

The little girl slowly got out of the car, then walked away.

Harrison glared at the cop. "I'm glad you stop these kidnaping perverts."

"It's what I was supposed to do."

"But that can't be procedure, can it? Asking a traumatized civilian to report in for you?"

"I don't know if it's standard procedure, and I don't care."

"You don't care?"

"I'm not a real cop." The rescuer, the Uniform Killer, had the length of rope out of the sleeve of his cop costume and around Harrison's neck before the journalist knew what was going on.

Not that Harrison Baker really knew. The serial murderer started to choke the life out of the journalist. Maybe the occult phenomenon Harrison had christened the Hotel of the Dead had, perhaps, never had a sinister design about it all—quite the opposite.

As he slipped out of this life and off to whatever comes next, Harrison Baker thought maybe the Hotel of the Dead had been kind of an early warning system.

Very early—like almost one's whole life early.

And, in Harrison Baker's case, that, pathetically, had still not been enough.

Expiation by L.J. Blount.

"Welcome, so pleased you could join me. Name's Benny, but then you probably already knew that." He said before flaming up a cigarette. Watching the burning cherry, he rolled the cigarette between his fingers and smiled smugly.

Teri sighed briefly, before sitting down on the grass across from him. She rolled her eyes in her mind she tried to draw to memory why it was exactly she agreed to the interview. Most happened over the Internet, indiscrete series of questions drawn out on her seventeen-inch monitor. Perhaps she thought this one would be different. Different because the Zine was local and one she had tried to publish with for what seemed like evermore to her. Besides, the atmosphere was nice. Grant Park on a sunny, not to warm early spring evening made for a nice setting. The sun was just moving behind the horizon and a slight easterly breeze brought with it the aroma of budding lilacs. She smiled, drawing a deep breath into her nostrils.

Mattered none. She was here, he was there, and the interview was just beginning. She braced herself for the same old questions. Where do you get your ideas, how long have you been writing, and who's your favorite author? Very imaginative questioning, very insightful for the reader as well, she thought. Yeah, as if they care who I read, she carped to herself.

Why, why did she do it? For years she has struggled to make it, all the while others seem to burst on the scene. She's read their wears and perhaps it is only envy, but she knows her talents are far more than theirs. Yet, they bathe in the accolades, the attention, and the paychecks. All the while she continues to struggle with free markets.

Teri grunted inside, tired and bitter from it all. Tired mostly, and sad perhaps more than anything.

"Yes?" She finally piped up as Benny continued to smirk at the burning cherry of his cigarette.

"What?" he shook his head as if drawn from a daydream.

Silence burned into the spring air. Teri watched a couple strolling hand and hand down a winding sidewalk. It was nice out she thought, trying to convince herself that she had made the right decision in agreeing to do the interview.

"Are you going to ask me a question or are we just going to sit here?" The question passed her lips after a long exhausted sigh.

She watched as Benny contorted his face into one of dismay, "You're not enjoying yourself?"

"The interview, we came here so you could interview me for the Zine." Teri stood, brushing her rear as she did.

"Whoa!" Taking a step back, she glared Benny down as he bolted from the ground.

"Sorry," he said, rubbing the back of his thigh. "Damn cramp."

"Look," Teri scanned the empty park. Feeling her nerves fray a bit, she summoned the courage to be brash. "I've been here the better part of twenty minutes and you haven't asked me a single question."

"Oh? A question?" Benny paced as he rubbed the small thatches of whiskers on his chin.

What an odd guy, she thought watching his face contort into painful expressions as he searched for a question. His short, almost dwarf frame jiggled like Jell-O as he wandered pointlessly before her.

"Ah!"

"Yes," Teri asked curiously.

"A question, I have a question for you." Benny said proudly.

"And?"

"Are you lonely for love?"

"What?"

"Love?"

"I, no! What the hell is this." Teri turned and started to walk away, waving her hand in an angry and abrupt good-bye.

"You asked me to ask you a question," Benny called to her.

"About my writing," Teri's words hung in park. She drew her hands to her ears covering them from the sting brought on by her sudden and thunderous echo.

"I care nothing about that," Benny said. Teri stepped back as he stood not a foot in front of her.

"How?" She asked. She peered behind her then swung her head back around. "How did . . ."

"There's no need for you to be rude. You came to me remember, I didn't seek you out."

She took another step back, fear told her to.

"I asked you a question, now you should respond."

"Who are you?"

Benny's lip curled into wicked smile, "Now you with the questions," he said as he chuckled beneath his breath.

"Who are you!"

"I fear you realize not what you have done by coming to me."

Teri turned away from Benny, "Fuck you," she said as she walked quickly away.

"There is no where for you to go now."

Teri's eyes welled as the sinister voice penetrated her. Somehow, she knew it was true. Somehow, she knew there was no where for her to run. There was no one in the park that could help her, even if there would have been people around. But the park was deserted and had been since she watched, longingly at the couple who strolled away from her hand-in-hand.

"You're not with the Zine are you?" Teri stopped, not bothering to turn and face him. She knew in time that he would make himself before her.

"I don't know what you are talking about." The sinister voice moved from her left, then stopped before her. Shortly there after, in the wake of the echo, he stood.

The tears rolled down her cheeks as the strange man peered menacingly at her. "You came to me," she heard him say; yet his lips didn't move.

Darkness fell upon the park. The early spring breeze quickly became a violent whipping wind as the greens of the park buckled beneath the grip of death.

Teri stood still as the world around her succumbed to another. An unfamiliar smell filled her nostrils, as the burn of the harsh air stung her delicate eyes. It was all around her, the unexplained, and the unimaginable. The terrain shifted from what was an even and rolling green firma, to a violent disarray. Dirt trails and tall trees gave way to jagged terrain, sunken vales, and molten soil. The heat that rose around her was unfamiliar as well, stinging, searing heat biting at her supple skin.

Then as it had changed once, it began again. A radiant light overtook the darkness, sending it beneath its veil. Great spiral staircases burst from the surface, sending a shower of earth into the boundless sky. The staircases reached for the Heavens, each garnished beautifully with ivory carvings and contrasting jade ivy. A calm assailed her, one she least expected in such a place as this. The ever-revolving atmosphere struck emotional disordered within, a disorder that was both alarming and enchanting.

"What do you want with me?" Teri asked, as her eyes widened in the wonderment before her.

"It is a tale of two. The good . . ."

Benny waved his short, hairy arm over his head.

Teri beamed at the sight of angels floating over her. Their gowns floated smoothly through the gentle breeze. Heavenly faces glowed radiantly, nearly invisible from the white light. She could see them though; the beauty of angels, their faces carried such serenity in them. Warmth filled her as she watched anxiously the angels as the reach of their wings embraced her.

She felt the touch of God against her. The forever feeling of love and belonging; home. There was no greater love than that she felt at that moment. No greater calm then that which soothed her soul as the wings of the angels cradled her in their radiant down.

"The bad . . ." Benny said menacingly, spreading his arms beneath him as he dipped before her.

As warm as the feeling was it soon melted away into an abhorred feeling of a thousand hands probing at her body. She looked down at the decomposing hands that scratched, poked, and pinched at her bare skin. She floated naked amidst a wave of demons that willingly shared in her flesh. Their moans of interest and ecstasy bit hard at her ears. The tears again flowed down her blush stained cheeks.

Teri screamed an empty cry for God. Her violent thrashes held in check by the ten thousand fingers that probed into her flesh, into her being. She fell, fell fast in the grasp of a thousand hands. She reached out from the pool of decomposing flesh, reached out for Benny. She looked up at him, his sunken eyes hollowed further into an abyss of nothingness. She could feel the emptiness of his heart as he peered down at her. Teri howled as she fell deeper.

She rose again no sooner she disappeared into the darkness, rose again on the wings of angels. The warmth was there, but diminished by betrayal. Her eyes, red, swollen from the tears she shed. Her skin carried welts from the pinching and probing cruel creatures, but quickly healed by the touch of the angels. She felt the warmth, but no longer safe. The angels stopped, lowering her gently to the ground before Benny.

The familiar landscape of the park returned to her. She was back to where it all began, back to where she first met Benny. She looked down at him; he reclined against a massive tree carrying the same smug smirk as before. "Who are you?" She asked, sniveling beneath a quivering breath.

Silence filled the park again. He did not respond, nor acknowledge her. She looked about; looked for someone she could call to; someone who might be willing to help her.

"They are all around you. They cannot see you, nor can you see them. In fact they are right next to you."

Teri reached out beside her, nothing. She looked again across the park but saw nothing.

Laughter drew her attention back to the man sitting unmoved at her feet. "I said they can't see you, as you can't see them. But I assure you they are there."

"Why? Who are they?"

"Others like you."

Teri fell to her knees. "Please tell me . . ."

Benny sighed jadedly, "They are others like you. Those who have journeyed beyond their world before their calling."

"You? Who are you?" Teri sank further down on her knees.

"I? I am Benny, or more formally Benziel. I am an Angel of God, a messenger, and the keeper. I am the keeper of this place, the place to where you have come." Benny smiled a devilish smile, "A place you have come of your own will."

"Angel?" Teri stood, shaking her head she turned and ran, ran as fast as her frightened legs would carry her. But like before she went no where, and like before her world morphed around her.

Demons and angels together, angels floated above her, demons slithering at her feet. "No!" She cried, "Where am I?"

The hands of demons snaked up her legs as the cries of angels rained down on her. Heaven and Hell were with her, together punishing her weary soul. The din grew to a near deafening clatter; she reached for the angels as the thousand hands of the demons pulled her into the earth.

A din rose, the clatter of clicking teeth of the demons and the flutter of angel wings intensified. Above this rose a thunderous voice; "You are in purgatory. Here is a place you will remain for a day, ten thousand days, or one hundred million days. A place you will remain until your Lord decides to judge your pitiful soul. Here with all the others like you, the takers of their own lives. Those who choose to throw away the gift of Christ. Heed, here I am your Lord the keeper of the domain, Purgatory. Here you remain, living in Heaven and Hell and the world you once inhabited. Here, until you are judged and I only pray it is for a long time so that I may have your soul to tease." A devilish laugh clapped like thunder across the angel raining sky as a thousand hands of hell pulled Teri beneath the earth.

"It's time for atonement," Benny smiled over the vale that held the tortured soul . . .

In a small apartment blood dripped from severed arteries. A woman's limp body slouched over a bloodied keyboard. Light from a monitor glistened against her auburn hair. On the monitor, a question blinks unassumingly, waiting for a response. "So, where do you get your ideas?" It asked, asked of a writer, asked of the dead.

After the Fall by Paul Fry

September 12th

Day one

We're lucky to be alive. Well, at least I think we are. My wife, Sandra, is very glad I built this shelter. I'm not so sure. Who knows what will be waiting for us when we surface again? That's if we ever do. We'll have to stay down here for at least two weeks, probably a lot longer. I don't know if we'll last that long. We'll probably go crazy.

Everything topside must be destroyed. It was a huge explosion. We nearly didn't get down here in time. The sirens started at about 11:30pm—I don't think there's any sound in the world worse than an air raid siren. Just thinking back to it now gives me chills.

When the sirens started, we were in the living room watching TV. At first we just looked at each other. I could see the fear in Sandra's eyes, she had always been afraid of a nuclear attack ever since she was a little girl. She use to have nightmares about it. That's why she'd pleaded with me to build this shelter. I didn't really think about it much.

Until now that is.

Now I can't stop thinking about it. I keep trying to remember all the things that I've heard and read about what supposed to happen after a nuclear attack. But I'm that afraid my mind can't recall very much, just the basics. I hope I can remember enough to keep us alive.

It's late now and we're both very tired. I'll continue with this diary tomorrow.

Day two

We had a very restless sleep. Sandra kept crying. I was awake most of the night comforting her. I'm afraid for her. I don't think she'll ever be the same again. She's changed. She was always happy before, but now, when she's not crying she just sits and stares into space. We don't speak much either. I try to hold a normal conversation—if you can call anything under these circumstances normal—but Sandra doesn't respond. She says the odd word now and again, but she doesn't make much sense. Perhaps she will get better in time. I hope so. I don't think I can bear to see her like this for much longer.

I started to keep a diary because there isn't much else to do. I have to do the daily checks of our shelter: check the air filter, make sure the seal on the hatch is intact, that sort of thing. But apart from that, there's nothing. I can't talk to Sandra and I'll go crazy if I don't keep busy.

I'm trying to think of things to write about, but my mind's a bit hazy. It's to be expected, though, I suppose.

I'll describe the shelter. That should give me plenty to write about.

I built it about four years ago. As I said earlier, Sandra wanted me to build it. I wasn't all that bothered really; I mean, who wants to survive a nuclear war? What's there to live for? If we had children then maybe that would give me a reason, but there again, who wants to see them suffer. The world will never be the same again. There's probably nothing left. I bet everything's gone. Still, I suppose somebody's got to survive and carry on. I don't see the point myself, but perhaps it's just me.

Anyway, back to the shelter.

It's one of those underground permanent shelters, made from twelve-inch thick reinforced concrete. It's about 15 feet long, 13 feet wide, and the ceiling's about 10 feet high. Not very big. Not big enough to be trapped in for two weeks anyway. Especially since I'm a bit claustrophobic. I hope I can take it. I've got no choice really; I've got to be strong for Sandra.

The inside of the shelter is very basic. There's a bed, a chemical toilet—that's not very pleasant, I'll tell you—along one wall, and there's a big box of supplies: food, water, toilet paper, first aid kit, can and bottle opener and knives and forks, that sort of thing, against the opposite wall. I've allowed enough food and water for about two weeks. I hope we don't have to stay down here any longer. It should be safe to go outside after two weeks. Maybe even sooner. It all depends on where the bombs landed.

Next to the supplies we've got a little table—well, actually it's an upturned box—with a portable radio on it. We've also got a spare radio, and some spare batteries. I haven't picked up anything yet. Perhaps the emergency broadcast system has been destroyed. But that's its job isn't it? It's supposed to broadcast during emergencies. I'll keep trying, but I don't want to waste the batteries. As soon as I receive anything, I'll write it down.

Oh yeah, we've also got a little box of tools next to our radio stuff. There's a screwdriver, hammer, a small shovel and a hatchet. Just in case we need them.

When I'd finished building the shelter, it looked like a prison cell. Concrete everywhere. The only thing that broke up the grayness of the concrete was the steel hatch in the ceiling, which I'd painted turquoise blue, just to give the place a little color.

Obviously, it isn't quite the same as a real prison cell. There isn't any metal bars caging you in, just concrete. But it's a lot worse than any prison cell I know of. In real prison you at least see some kind of daylight. Not here. This shelter is like a sealed box. No daylight gets in anywhere. The only light comes from torches that we position around the shelter.

Sandra's put up a few posters on the walls to try and make it look cozier. I'm looking at the one above me as I write. It's a picture of the New York skyline. I've always wanted to go to New York to see the Statue of Liberty. It's probably not there anymore.

I'm starting to feel a little depressed. I think I'll stop writing for today. I'll be back tomorrow.

Day five

Things are getting worse. Sandra's more withdrawn. She hasn't spoken for days, and I don't feel well. Maybe the air filter isn't working properly. I'll take a look at it. If it *isn't* working correctly, were fucked. We'll have to take our chances topside. It might not be so bad actually; there may be people up there. It's got to be better than being stuck in this little box. That's what it feels like anyway, a box. It's starting to look smaller every day. I'd say the walls are closing in, but that's not really possible, is it? I don't think so.

Day seven

I feel worse. I've got the shakes and my head hurts.

Sandra's dead. She wouldn't eat. I tried to feed her, but she kept spitting it out. I kept shoving the food back in, but I must have shoved in too much. She started choking. Anyway, she was getting on my nerves. She just sat there and stared at the wall all day long.

She's starting to smell a bit. I don't think I can stay down here much longer.

Day ten

I can't take the smell any longer. I've got to get out of here.

Day twelve

I'm back. I had to leave the shelter. I got rid of Sandra while I was up there. It's not so bad down here now. I like it. It's peaceful and quiet, and I can pop up for some fun whenever I feel like it.

I had a lot of fun yesterday. Fell over and cracked my fucking head, though. That wasn't fun. It hurt like shit. There's fucking rubble everywhere. I was right, everything's destroyed. My house is gone.

Everything's gone.

Not everyone's dead though.

Almost everyone.

I managed to find a nice looking girl. She was a bit burnt, a little mangled, but not too bad.

I fucked her. Several times, in fact. She didn't put up a fight at all. I was a bit disappointed really; it's not the same when they just lie there. She moved when I stabbed her, though. She put up a fight then. Tried her best, anyway. She kicked and screamed a lot. I couldn't work out what she was saying, though. A bunch of gurgles. That probably had a lot to do with the steel rod I jammed down her throat.

After I'd had my fun with Spike (that's what I nicknamed her), I roamed around for a few hours. I didn't see anybody else. I'll go out again tomorrow. Maybe I'll have more luck then.

Day fourteen

What a time I've had! I nearly didn't make it back. Some fucking lunatic attacked me. I was scouting around for women, men, I don't care anymore, when this crazy bastard jumped up from a hole in the ground and bashed me over the head with a fucking leg. Can you believe it. He actually hit me with a human limb. It fucking hurt. Left a fucking bump on the side of my head. A fucking leg.

I might try that one myself. I could use an arm (watch out, I'm armed) . . . or even better, a head. I could tie some rope around it and use it like a club. I could swing the fucker around and bash the shit out of someone with it.

Hey you, how about a little head?

I could use Sandra's head. She's still up there.

I hope.

It should be easy to cut her head off. She's been up there a couple of days now. She's got to be rotten.

I'll have a look around for some rope, I'll go up and see if I can find her. I'll take the hatchet from the box of tools. I should be able to chop her head off nicely with that.

It's off to work I go!

Day Fifteen

It worked a treat. I managed to find Sandra's body. Some crazy bastard had dragged her away and started to eat her, if you can believe that. Most of her lower body and legs were missing. They probably went first because they were the fattiest parts of her. Saying that though, her tits were still intact. A bit rotten, but still intact, and they were huge. Loads of fat there if that's what the crazy fucker was after.

When I found her, she was spread-eagle on top of some rubble. Part of an old table or something. Even though she was rotten and not totally intact, she didn't look too bad. I even thought about fucking her one last time. I decided against the idea, though. Sandra didn't like me to fuck her when she was alive. I could imagine what she'd think if I fucked her while she was like that. I know she's dead, but I still thought better of it.

I positioned myself above her and gave her a final kiss good-bye, then I chopped her head off. It came off easier than I expected it would. Someone had tried before me, I think. God only knows why. There are some sick fuckers in this world.

I'd just managed to get her head off and get the rope tied around it when someone attacked me from behind.

She didn't expect my retaliation, though. I swung Sandra's head at her. She screamed even before it made contact. The first blow didn't kill her. It just knocked her down and dazed her a bit. Gave me time to fuck her.

This one didn't just lie there like old Spike had. She put up a hell of a fight until I buried my hatchet in her forehead.

After I fucked her, I got myself a little idea. The sight of the hatchet protruding from her head is what gave it to me. My first attempt at a 'head-club' hadn't worked so well, so I decided to try something new. I scouted around for some nails or anything long and sharp. It took me a while to find something that would do the trick, but I finally found an old tool kit in the ruins of someone's garage. Some good shit had survived the blast.

I found some six-inch nails. I couldn't find a hammer, but the flat side of my hatchet worked just as well. I knocked a few nails into Sandra's head, leaving about three inches of each nail sticking out. When I finished with her, she looked a bit like Pinhead from that old movie *Hellraiser*.

I was off again.

I got me quite a few people that day. Had some real fun. Lately, though, I've begun to feel sick. I've decided to stay here in the shelter for a few days. Maybe that'll help.

Day Eighteen

I'm not getting any better.

I tried to go out yesterday but didn't quite make it. After a lot of effort, I managed to open the shelter's hatch. I'd just struggled to get my head and upper body outside when I saw a group of people lurking behind a big pile of rubble not far from my shelter. There were about four of them. They were hunched over something that sort of resembled a person. They were tugging and pulling at it. I think they were eating someone. I must have gasped or made some kind of noise. One of them turned and looked in my direction.

I saw blood all around his mouth. It contrasted bright against unnatural grayness of his skin.

I think he saw me. I mean, I don't know if he actually *saw* me, but he looked *at* me. His movements were slow and sluggish, and as I said, his skin was a very pale gray color. He must have been exposed to a lot of fallout. He looked ill. He looked dead, actually. That isn't possible, though. The dead don't walk, right?

The way he looked at me made me shudder. I returned to the safety of my shelter and locked myself in.

I think they're trying to get me. I've heard muffled voices—more like groans actually—and strange sounds all night.

It's five in the morning now. They've been at it nonstop for hours.

I just heard the hatch creak.

I've got my hatchet and my 'head-club' ready. Maybe Sandra will help me.

Then again . . . after what I did to her, maybe not.

Biographies

Mike Bohatch

Mike@eyesofchaos.com

Being involved in the arts in one form or another for most of my life, it was my passion for horror movies and a fascination for bizarre imagery that led me to illustration. While working over 7 years in the digital field in the areas of print, design, prepress, and color correction, it wasn't until implementing my studies of traditional fine arts that I began to bring true realization of my ideas and visions by combining the physical side of fine arts with the digital realm of computer graphics. With this mindset began a unique image-making process I refer to as "digital organics".

Currently I am specializing in horror and dark, surreal, metaphysical illustration, combining a mixture of drawing, painting, collage, photography, and digital compositing. Work includes: CD art, magazine illustrations and covers, comic covers, and motion graphics.

Carl Hose

maskedwriter@msn.com

Carl Hose lives in St. Louis, Missouri. He is the father of two kids, an avid movie fan, and a constant writer. His publishing credits include adult magazines, horror magazines, a bunch of e-zines, and Lighthouse Digest. He is the creator and keeper of the Writer's Inkwell web site.

Walt Hicks

wwhicks@hotmail.com

Walt Hicks lives on the Treasure Coast of Florida. He is married with twin girls and works as the accounting manager for an aerospace firm. A writer for nearly 30 years, Walt has been extensively published on the internet and is the editor/publisher of the monthly speculative fiction e-zine "DeathGrip".

Paul Melniczek

MrZek@aol.com

Small business owner who teaches part time at a college. Started writing earlier this year and have written stories in the horror, speculative, general, and science fiction genres. Hope to work and complete two novels this year and have many works circulating in the market, a growing amount coming to publication already. I enjoy writing and the challenges it presents. Married with two children. Hobbies include the outdoors, music, and several sports activities.

Horns

horns9@hotmail.com

Horns. Born & raised in Ohio, I started writing a little over a year ago. The genesis of my interest in horror, from my earliest memories, stems from a time when the ‘Drive-in’ was as popular as our modern multiplex theaters. Today, I love trying to hunt down horror films from the fragments of the images my mind, as a child, committed to memory. To this day, I remain an avid fan of the great television shows such as HBO’s: Tales from the Crypt, The Twilight Zone, Friday the 13th the Series, Outer Limits, and Tales from the Darkside, to name but a few. I have a great number of other interests that I will not bore you with here. Suffice it to say, *HORROR* is in my blood . . . want to see? Muhahahaha!

Steven E. Wedel

moon_howler@yahoo.com

Steven E. Wedel was born in April 1966 in Stillwater, Oklahoma. He grew up in Enid, Oklahoma and married his junior high sweetheart in 1985. He first dreamed of being a writer when he enrolled in Wilda Walkers “Creative Writing” class at Enid High School. However, after graduation he spent 10 years working in machine shops before going to college to earn a degree saying he could write. Steve now lives in Oklahoma City with his wife and two kids—with a third coming in October—and works for The Daily Oklahoman newspaper, where his editors ask that he save the horror fiction for his spare time.

Amy Grech

agrech@crimsonscreams.com

Amy Grech is a 28 year old writer who has had work appear in: 69 Flavors of Paranoia, Alexandria Digital Literature (twice), Altered Perceptions Magazine, Blue Murder Magazine, Classic Pulp Fiction Stories, The Darklands Project Issue #1, Dark Muse, Dueling Minds, Funeral Party 2, Gathering Darkness, Gallery, Hoodz, House of Pain, Massacre, Nasty Snips, Penny Dreadful, Pulp Fiction Magazine, Short, Scary Tales, and Weird Stories.

Stories are forthcoming in: DeathGrip, Fears Mag.Com, The Haunted, Songs of Innocence, and Tourniquet Heart. Her story, “A Splash of Crimson”, which appeared in Nasty Snips, received a Stoker nomination. Visit her web site: www.crimsonscreams.com, for a good fright.

Kevin James Miller

kevinjamesmiller@hotmail.com

Over fifty of Kevin James Miller's stories, reviews, and poems have appeared in over twenty on-line publications. Visit his Web site, "Beyond the Real: The Fiction of Kevin James Miller," at http://www.webspawner.com/users/kjmiller. He will soon have a story in Suspect Thoughts. He's currently a college teacher, and he's also been, among other things, an usher, factory worker, film projectionist, and door-to-door salesman.

L.J. Blount

myth_spinner@yahoo.com

L.J. Blount (also known as Myth Spinner) has over thirty short horror and fantasy tales in print and making the rounds over the Internet. Visit his web site at www.geocities.com/myth_spinner for more information about his short fiction and other literary projects. "Myth" currently calls Colorado home.

Paul Fry

paul@shortscarytales.com

Paul began writing horror stories in August of '99. His love of reading short stories and novels by great authors such as Richard Laymon, Ray Garton, Bentley Little, Graham Masterton, David J. Schow, Rex Miller, and George R.

R. Martin, spans back over a decade. It was his passion for reading horror stories that gave him the urge to write.

He was born and still lives in Birmingham, England, but would love to one day live in his favourite place in the world, Florida.

Lightning Source UK Ltd.
Milton Keynes UK
21 December 2009

147800UK00001B/123/A

9 781929 072675